# "You said I should hire someone . . ."

She'd been on the delivering end of the same argument with Roxie the night before and knew just what to say. "My roommate has the skills we need, and we worked together in—" now wasn't the time to mention her own days in the circus "—other capacities," she finished lamely. "Believe me, she's qualified,"

Reid's glance slid over her in slow appraisal. Something about his intent regard tugged at her, and for a long pulsing moment she tried to read his changing signals.

He straightened, and the signals were gone. "Just remember, you're responsible for her work."

Kathryn's mind struggled to change direction. "Yes, of—of course," she stammered. The naked and complex honesty of that one look from him had unnerved her, as did the echo of Roxie's reassurances—*Kath, what could possibly go wrong!*

**Patricia Knoll**, "when facing the imminent arrival of birthday number thirty and baby number four," decided there had to be more to life than changing diapers. She produced her first Harlequin Romance a few years later. Raised in a copper-mining town in the American West, she's always been fascinated by interesting characters and the stories they have to tell. And she's always loved books—the things with "new worlds to become lost in." Now she creates new worlds, too—ones with love and humor and happy endings.

# Send in the Clown

## Patricia Knoll

# Harlequin Books

TORONTO • NEW YORK • LONDON
AMSTERDAM • PARIS • SYDNEY • HAMBURG
STOCKHOLM • ATHENS • TOKYO • MILAN

ISBN 0-373-03002-9

Harlequin Romance first edition September 1989

This book is dedicated to
Pat Cooney, who worked on it as hard as I did.

My thanks go to Don Gonsalves,
Dee Gee the Clown,
who taught me a few tricks of his trade.

# CHAPTER ONE

HER CAR had seen her leaving the office. Kathryn just knew it. The fifteen-year-old Buick had sat demurely in the parking lot for the past ten hours with all its mysterious parts in perfect working order.

The instant she had stepped from the building, locked the door behind her, dashed out in the pouring rain—minus umbrella—and tumbled into the front seat, the car had decided to have a breakdown. She tried the motor again and again, but her efforts only met with a grinding sound, and even that was pitifully weak.

Twisting on the worn blue vinyl of the seat, Kathryn looked back at the building that housed Tucson Janitorial Supplies. The parking lot was empty, and as far as she knew everyone was gone. The warehouse night crew wouldn't be coming for another hour, and she couldn't wait that long. She was going to have to go back into the building and call a tow truck—which might not arrive anyway because all such services were presently overburdened thanks to the arrival of Arizona's annual rain and flood season.

Kathryn hooked thick, wet curls of coppery red hair behind her ears, rubbed her palms over her cheeks and sighed a long breath, then rested her forehead against the steering wheel. The aching tensions she had been fighting all day crawled up the back of her neck and began to pound in her head.

These past two days may not have been the worst of her life, but they ranked somewhere in the top five. She squeezed her eyes so tightly shut that her lashes disappeared in the folds of her lids. She was exhausted, and all she wanted to do was get home and sink into a hot bath.

She pushed away from the steering wheel and folded her arms in self-comfort across the waist of her damp, crumpled dress. Her stomach felt as if it was kinked and gnarled like twists of old barbed wire. A deep restorative breath might have helped, but the car's interior was sultry and airless. It had baked through Tucson's morning heat, then been blasted by the latest edition of the monsoonlike express.

She was hot, sticky, tired, and more than a little angry. Suddenly, she slammed a palm against the steering wheel.

It wasn't fair, she thought, letting indignation rise and swamp her for a minute. She had done her best. For six months she had worked as hard as possible for TJS. Maybe her position wasn't very important. Junior secretaries, even ones filling in as executive assistant to the president, were pretty low on the totem pole, but she had tried hard, and the company's president, Reid Darwin, hadn't shown any recognition or appreciation.

Kathryn's green-gold eyes glittered. Appreciation. Ha! Reid Darwin hadn't even called her by name until she had worked for his company three months! Naively, she had thought yesterday's events would change that. That just showed how wrong a person could be!

She caught a glimpse of herself in the rearview mirror and wrinkled her short nose. All right, maybe recognition and appreciation had been too much to ask.

A flex of her shoulders pulled her away from the seat, and the skin exposed by her sundress made a soft sucking sound as it left the vinyl. Maybe she was making too much of it, she thought, absently rubbing her damp neck. Everyone else at TJS liked her, appreciated the work she did, thought of her as a professional.

It was possible that she simply wasn't Reid's idea of an executive secretary, even a temporary one. She did tend to wear casual styles rather than suits, but that could change. Her thick red hair had a mind of its own, tangling and flying about her face, but she would tame it, if she had to use a whip and chair! It couldn't be her looks, she thought, touching her damp cheeks. There wasn't much to dislike about the regular features and small pointed chin that gave her face a heart shape. Her fingers came away dotted with running mascara, and she was glad the owner of TJS couldn't see her right then.

Nor was Reid Darwin the type to bully someone just because she was a full twelve inches shorter than he was—but there was something wrong with her.

A thought occurred to her and she caught her own glance in the mirror, a rueful smile lifting the corners of her eyes. Perhaps she was just spoiled. In her previous job she had been adored by thousands.

Cheered by that memory she fought back the resentment she felt and leaned forward to try the ignition once again. The grinding sound from under the hood reconfirmed that the car wasn't going anywhere unless towed. She shrugged.

Feeling like a diver going underwater, Kathryn inhaled a deep breath of the car's muggy air, pulled the strap of her shoulder bag up and reached for the door handle. At any other time she might not have minded the rain—it was such a glorious display of nature's power. But today was different.

The instant she stepped out of the car, she was once again drenched, her yellow cotton dress clinging like a banana peel. Head down, she began splashing through the now ankle-deep water, her feet slipping inside her high heels and forcing her to take slow, careful steps. Over the din of the pouring rain, she could hear a heavier rushing sound. Blinking against the torrent, she turned her head.

Reid Darwin's Jeep Cherokee was bearing down on her.

Rats! Kathryn scowled. She didn't want him to see her like this. She didn't want to see him again today at all. He must have been parked around the end of the building. She had thought he was already gone.

Head down again, she quickened her pace, almost losing her footing where the asphalt dipped near the storm drain. The water swirling into it looked like a whirlpool, and for a moment she experienced a nauseating vertigo, fearing she would be swept down with it.

Her wet fingers groped for her keys as she tried to make it back to the office door. Reid honked his car horn, and his hand shot out to motion her to him.

Kathryn shook her head. Thunder clapped overhead and she looked up fearfully. A blast of rain and wind hit her directly in the face, and she dashed her hand across her eyes.

Reid pulled up beside her, his voice booming out, "Need help?"

He was the last person she wanted help from. "No," she shouted over the sound of the pelting rain, hating the situation, wishing he would just go away. "I'm going to call a tow truck."

"Your car won't start?"

She shook her head again and was about to turn her back to him.

He reached across to open the Jeep's door for her, one powerful thrust pushing it wide, and immediately rain began to darken the upholstery inside the vehicle. "Get in!"

"No. I'm already drenched." Kathryn shouted the excuse as she backed away, one hand in front of her.

He straightened and jerked his thumb toward the rider's side, looking ready to lunge out after her. "Damn it, get in the car!"

Deciding it wasn't worth arguing about, she dashed around the car, tumbled in and slammed the door.

He gave her a frowning look as he rolled the window up to keep the rain out and the blessed dryness in. He didn't say anything for a moment as his eyes skimmed over her.

Kathryn met his gaze straight on, hiding her irritation that he appeared untouched by the storm while she resembled a drowned rat.

The man was like a pillar of granite, she thought, exasperated. Six feet, four inches tall, with big shoulders and arms, he dwarfed most men. His hair was the color of tobacco ripening in the sun. His jaw was long and square, his nose high-bridged and prominent, his brows bushy and darker than his hair. She noticed he'd removed the jacket of his lightweight suit, as well as

his tie, and had rolled up the sleeves of his white shirt
to expose muscled forearms dusted with hair.

Comparing her disarray to his neat appearance,
Kathryn grimaced, feeling uncomfortably aware of her
red hair tumbling in sodden strands around her
shoulders. Her pretty cotton dress, with the intricate
Mexican embroidery across the bodice, looked like a
limp dishrag, and her running eye makeup made her
resemble a drunken raccoon. Shivering, she arranged
the wet folds of her skirt and tried to unobtrusively
pluck the dress top away from where it was plastered
to her breasts.

Reid flipped the air conditioner vents away from her
and, turning, reached behind the seat to pull a blanket forward. "Here. Now will you please tell me what
happened?"

"My car won't start," she answered, wrapping his
scratchy stadium blanket around herself, silently
blessing its warmth. It was quite a day for contrasts.

His direct look told her not to state the obvious.

"I was going back inside to call a tow truck." Feeling curious, she looked around at the rich upholstery
and the clean square lines of the Jeep's interior. She
had seen her boss driving it but had never glimpsed the
inside before. The utilitarian-looking vehicle with its
surprisingly plush interior suited him.

"You could have waited until the night crew came
on. Someone would have helped you."

She shot him an impatient look, knowing she would
already be calling for a truck if he hadn't stopped her.
"I'm in a hurry to get home."

Reid considered her for another moment, seemed to
come to a swift decision and reached for the gearshift. "I'll take you. Where do you live?"

Alarm caused her to jerk up straight, and her arms came out of the blanket. "That isn't necessary."

"I said, I'll take you home," he answered in a mild voice, rocklike determination underlying it. "Why the hurry, anyway?" He turned his head to face her. "Is someone special waiting for you?"

His personal question took her so much by surprise that she answered without thinking. "Yes, there is, as a matter of fact." Bosco went berserk during thunderstorms, and it would probably take her half an hour to find him when she got home. "I have to see about my dog," she blurted.

His square jaw sagged in surprise and his eyes widened, amusement flickering in them. "You're rushing home through a rainstorm because of a *dog*!"

She shivered again and rubbed her thick hair with a corner of the blanket. Bosco was one reason for hurrying home, but mainly she wanted to escape the man at her side, to sit quietly for a moment after her hectic day and try to decide how she was going to handle the extra work she'd taken on. "He needs me. He's afraid of thunder," she explained, earning an even more incredulous look from him.

"Most dogs are," he pointed out.

"Well, Bosco is special," she said, drawing the blanket around her. Why had she said such a thing? She could just as easily have told him she had to hurry home to sick parents. He didn't know they had turned their house over to her, retired from their teaching jobs and moved to Springerville in the White Mountains. And he certainly didn't know they were in very good health.

"Special because he's yours?"

"Yes—and someone I used to work with gave him to me," Kathryn said. Wanting suddenly to give a little more information about her remarkable pet, she added, "He's afraid of thunder because it sounds so much like cannon fire."

He whipped his head toward her, his bushy brows shooting up high. "Cannon fire! What goes on at your place?"

She hadn't intended to get into details, and before she could explain, a blast of rain hit the Jeep and he had to give all his attention to driving. Scores of abandoned cars came into view when they pulled onto the street.

The water reached the doors on most vehicles. Kathryn looked around nervously at the number of motorists who were abandoning their cars and plodding through the rain. The Cherokee moved slowly, competently, and she saw Reid relax a bit into his seat. She watched the way his big hands eased off in their grip on the steering wheel, and she tried to relax, too.

"Where do you live?"

"Raymond Road. It's on—" her voice lowered in despair "—the other side of Cienega Wash."

He frowned. "Which is full of runoff from the Rillito River. Your dog may have a late dinner tonight."

Kathryn gulped. Her dog might have a mistress floating down Cienega Wash! "Do you think we should try walking?"

He grimaced as the Jeep shimmied through puddles that hid ruts. "What's the matter? Don't trust me?"

"It's the flood I don't trust!"

"We'll do fine," he said through gritted teeth, fighting the steering wheel as they entered an intersection where a rush of water hit the Jeep.

Kathryn gripped the door handle and closed her eyes, but after a few seconds, she opened them again. If something was going to happen in this flood, it would happen whether her eyes were open or closed. She caught a glimpse of Reid's expression as he darted a glance her way. It wavered between amusement and disbelief.

"Try to relax," he muttered.

Feeling foolish, she lifted her chin above the blanket folds but didn't answer. After a moment, he said, "Jill called just before I left the office."

Turning immediately, Kathryn put out her hand. Whether to stave off bad news about her boss or to pull forth good, she didn't know. "How is she? Has something happened?" She couldn't keep the tremor from her voice.

Reid looked chagrined, as if realizing how his abrupt announcement had sounded. "No, she just wanted to say she's being released from the hospital soon. She and the baby are stabilized, so she can go home." His voice was pitched to soothe her.

A shaky smile curved Kathryn's lips. "To spend the next three months in bed. She's going to be bored and restless."

"But she'll save her baby," Reid said quickly.

"Of course," Kathryn answered. She might have taken offense at his abrupt tone if she hadn't known how worried he had been about Jill. Their relationship went beyond boss and executive assistant. Jill and Reid were friends.

As Kathryn and Reid would never be. She shifted uncomfortably at the thought.

Momentarily she knew again the utter terror she had felt yesterday when she'd walked into the office she shared with Jill Clevenger, Kathryn's boss and Reid Darwin's right hand.

Jill had been doubled over her desk as if she'd been rising from her chair when the pain hit. One violently trembling arm on the desktop supported her while the other cradled the bulge of the six-month pregnancy she'd carried so proudly.

With a gasp of dismay Kathryn hurried to help her. "Jill, what's wrong?"

Pleading, pain-filled eyes turned to her. "Kathryn, it hurts. The baby. Help me."

"Yes, yes, of course." Kathryn eased Jill back into her chair, then swung away and dashed down the hall to Reid Darwin's office, instinct telling her that he could be counted on to deal with the problem.

He was on the phone when she barreled into his office, her face frantic and her hair flying wildly around her head. Before she could get her breath, he dropped the phone and surged to his feet. "What is it?"

"Jill. I think she's going into labor!"

He didn't waste any time on unnecessary questions but hurried with her back to his secretary's office. He bent over Jill, murmuring questions and reassurances, his big blunt fingers touching her tenderly.

"I'm going to have Kathryn call your doctor," Reid said. "What's the number, Jill?"

Concentrating on each digit Jill panted out the number.

Kathryn called, told the nurse she was bringing Jill in and hung up. Taking a deep breath she said, "I think you'll have to do without us this afternoon, Reid.''

His look was swift and decisive. "The company will have to do without all three of us. I'll drive. You come along to hold Jill's hand." He clipped out the orders then smiled at Jill. "I'll go slowly, but if I jar you, just slug me."

She gave him a shaky smile. "Gladly." Another pain hit her, paling her face. "Please hurry."

Kathryn dashed around, gathering up their purses. Reid picked Jill up in his powerful arms as if she weighed no more than a child and was as fragile as old parchment. He carried her to his Chrysler New Yorker, waited while Kathryn unlocked the back door, then slid Jill inside and fastened her seat belt. Kathryn hurried around and clambered in beside her.

Gently Reid touched his fingers to Jill's sweat-beaded forehead, and Kathryn was mesmerized by the tenderness in his face. He assured Jill that everything would be all right, and Kathryn at least believed him.

Reid rounded the car, climbed into the driver's seat, started the engine, then hooked his right elbow over the seat and glanced over his shoulder as he prepared to back the car out.

Kathryn's eyes darted up to his, holding there while shared fear passed between them. She knew her expression was anxious, but Reid's held anguish she couldn't begin to analyze. Responding to it, she reached out to touch his arm. "It's going to be all right," she said. "You just said so."

"Let's hope." He mouthed the words, adding in a loud reassuring tone, "Hold on."

She nodded, clasping Jill's hand as he shot out of the parking lot.

Later, in the private hospital room Reid had insisted on booking, the two women clutched hands as they waited for Jill's husband to arrive. Across the room Reid sat in a too-small chair, looking as if he would rather be pacing. Whenever Jill looked in his direction, though, he murmured words of encouragement or offered a comforting smile.

"The doctor says everything will be fine if you stay in bed and rest for the remainder of your pregnancy," Kathryn reminded her boss gently.

"I know," Jill said. "We've waited seventeen years for this baby. I'm not taking any risks, but I don't know what to do about work. We've barely started on those data processing manuals and . . ."

Kathryn's hand shot forward to smoothe the hair back from Jill's damp face. "Don't worry about a thing. You're not supposed to fret. I'll look after your job."

Jill's brown eyes filled with tears. "Oh, Kathryn, do you think you can do it?"

"Of course. I've had a wonderful teacher." She had spoken without thinking, hoping to relieve the anxiety in Jill's eyes, and she hoped it was the right thing to do.

She glanced up when Reid's feet scraped the tile floor. A swift frown of displeasure creased his forehead before Jill turned her face to him. His expression cleared instantly.

"Is that all right with you, Reid?" Jill asked.

"Of course. Don't worry about a thing. Why don't you close your eyes and rest now?" His voice was soothing, prompting Jill to do as he advised, but the hard look he gave Kathryn put the lie to his assurances.

She'd thought he would be glad, even grateful, that she was willing to take over and ease Jill's worries—and to make life easier for him—but on the way back to the office in his car Reid had questioned her abilities and coolly put her on a thirty-day performance review, as if she'd just walked in off the street!

Even now, in the safety of his Jeep, Kathryn still felt hurt by Reid's announcement of his lack of faith in her.

Kathryn tried to concentrate on the passing scenes, the stranded cars and motorists, the snail's pace of the traffic, but her resentment of the previous day spilled out.

She turned to face him, bracing her shoulders against the door as if spoiling for a fight. "I *can* do Jill's job, you know," she said, her voice low and fierce, her hands balled into fists. "I type fast and take shorthand almost as well as Jill does. I've been Jill's assistant for six months, so I know a little bit about your company."

Reid's head jerked around, showing his surprise at her outburst. He surveyed her for a moment before answering, and she felt as though he was cataloging the spots of color that rode high on her cheeks and the militant glint in her eyes. Without warning his lips spread in one of his rare, genuine smiles. "Believe it or not, your skills aren't in question, Kathryn." She knew the effect of his words showed in the widening of her eyes before he pulled his attention back to the street.

"Then what is it?" she demanded.

"Look at it from my standpoint," he went on in a reasonable tone. "You're still new at the company, you've only been with us a short time. Most of what I do is confidential. I have to expect professionalism in all areas—''

"And one afternoon you caught me salsa dancing in the employee lounge with one of the sales reps."

Their gazes tangled, and Kathryn's dropped first. She relived the moment when the sales rep had bent her back over his arm at the worst possible angle and Reid Darwin had walked in. Even from her upside-down position, she hadn't been able to mistake Reid Darwin's frown for a smile. In fact, he'd looked as if he wanted to jerk her up off the floor and fire her on the spot.

"The man was depressed about breaking up with his girlfriend, and I just wanted to cheer him up." At Reid's sidelong look, her voice faded. She cleared her throat and went on. "I promise I won't let anything like that happen again," she said primly, her fingers twisting in the scratchy wool blanket. The incident had made her appear flighty and silly, she knew, something she couldn't afford right now.

Determination settled inside her. She would simply have to show him that his suspicions were unfounded. There was no doubt she could do the job Jill was counting on her to do.

She could feel his gaze on her again, and she looked up to meet it. He seemed to read the resolve in her face and reacted with a raised brow. "Then we should get along just fine."

He reached over and flipped on the radio, to catch the weather report, he said, but the lightning-induced static was so strong he had to shut it off. With a sideways glance at Kathryn he shoved a Rita Coolidge cassette into his tape player.

While the singer's silk-over-sandpaper voice filled the Jeep, Kathryn leaned back to continue the ride in silence, her mind forming and discarding pithy remarks she would like to make to the man beside her.

It took almost an hour, but finally they reached Cienega Wash, where a public safety officer stopped them.

The man's muffled voice came from beneath his plastic-covered ranger-type hat as he spoke to Reid. "Sorry, sir, you can't proceed unless you can prove you live in the area."

"I don't, officer, but the lady does."

Kathryn fought her way out of the confining blanket and produced her driver's license.

The officer studied it carefully, handed it back and looked at Reid. "I have to advise you that even though you've got a four-wheel-drive vehicle, it's very dangerous to drive across the bridge. Most people are walking."

Reid and Kathryn looked ahead. A thick rope was stretched along the bridge to give the pedestrians an extra handhold.

Kathryn felt slightly ill as she looked down at the swirling brown water. The dry wash that had been lined with mesquite and acacia bushes was clogged with a huge pile of brush and uprooted trees. Several trash cans, and even a doghouse, were piled up against one of the far corners of the bridge. Water was running over the bridge as well as under it.

"You don't have to go on." Kathryn pressed her face to the window and watched the floodwaters, thinking that he probably couldn't wait to dump her. He couldn't have guessed that his offer of a ride was going to turn into one of the adventures of a lifetime!

She was anxious to get away. Home, she thought with longing, a hot bath, her robe and a few minutes of soothing her dog were what she wanted.

"I can hold on to that rope and go on alone." Just as she spoke, a man crossing the bridge lost his footing and flailed at the rope. A safety officer slogged forward to help him.

"Sure you can," Reid said, his wide mouth twisting upward. "But how about if you just humor me and let me see you home, okay? How far is it to Raymond Road from here?"

Once again the choice was being wrested from her. "Four blocks."

He nodded. One big hand slipped the gearshift into reverse as he turned to check traffic behind him. "Fine. We'll park the Jeep and go ahead on foot. I'll come back for it."

This was becoming impossible. She wanted to argue further but knew it would be pointless.

He parked the vehicle, pulled two rain ponchos from the back seat and threw one in her lap. "Better cover up and take off your shoes." He glanced down at her three-inch heels. "I don't suppose you have anything as practical as a pair of boots in that bag, do you?" he asked, indicating her large tote.

She shook her head.

"Umbrella?"

Kathryn shook her head again, then ducked down to remove her shoes and stuff them into her bag. Her imagination supplied the disgusted sigh he probably wanted to release.

Without a word he indicated that she should put on one of the ponchos as he was doing. They slid out of the Jeep and Kathryn nearly gagged when she stepped ankle-deep in mud. The rain was finally beginning to let up, which made the situation a little more bearable, but she grimaced with each step. The mud was bad enough, but it also hid the rocks, pebbles and twigs that were lying in wait to torture her feet.

He met her at the front of the vehicle and glanced downward. She lifted one foot. The tattered remains of her panty hose were plastered to her feet by an inch-thick coating of muck.

"It's too dangerous for you to go barefoot—and you can't wear those heels." He turned his broad back to her and crouched with his hands on his knees. "Climb on. I'll have to carry you."

Panicked, Kathryn backed up against the Jeep. "Carry me! But... but... I... No!"

"There's no other way, Miss Evans," he said, twisting his neck to look at her. His square jaw was set, and he was regarding her as if he thought she was overreacting. He jerked his head in summons. "Come on, we're wasting time."

Kathryn gazed at him in dismay. Having him rescue her in the parking lot had been embarrassing enough, but this was undoubtedly the worst moment of her life. Dread twisted in her like a giant fist. She really didn't want to do this, but she had no choice. Reluctantly she turned around and stepped up on the Jeep's bumper. "I think, Mr. Darwin, that under the circumstances you could call me Kathryn," she said with stiff dignity made ludicrous by her bedraggled appearance.

He looked at her, obviously fighting a grin. "*I'm* the one *under* the circumstances, so you'd better call me Reid."

Kathryn blinked, amazed that this man had actually made a joke. He tried to help her get onto his back by hooking his hands under her knees, but his poncho was still wet. Kathryn had to scramble for a handhold and finally leaned all the way forward to stretch her arms around his massive shoulders, clasping her hands in front of his throat.

She fervently hoped that no one they knew would see them.

Despite the awkwardness of the moment, she was all too conscious of what it was like to have his hands, impersonal though his grip on her was, wrapped around the backs of her knees. She told herself it was only because she was so wet and miserable that his touch seemed unusually warm.

He held her easily, but she felt as though her arms were almost pulled out of their sockets as she tried to hang on to his shoulders. Her chin was practically resting on his shoulder, and her nose was buried in the thick tobacco-brown hair at the back of his neck. Spicy after-shave, freshened by the rain, teased her sense of smell.

Kathryn turned her face, shrinking away from the kind of awareness that was forcing itself on her.

Reid felt her movement and his hold tightened on her. Tingling sensations shot up the backs of her legs to land in her stomach like one of the lightning bolts crackling in the distance. She gulped in a breath, and Reid jerked his head around.

"What's the matter?"

"N-nothing," she said, her voice catching. "Just the lightning."

He frowned, the steel-gray eye nearest her narrowing skeptically.

He has the longest eyelashes, Kathryn thought helplessly. She tilted her head to get a better look. Thick and full, too.

Under her hands, Kathryn could feel the slow, steady beat of his heart. Her own, pressed between his shoulder blades, began to pound like the beat of cicada wings.

When he became aware of her fascinated regard, Reid turned his head even farther until their eyes met. His were shuttered, not allowing her to read his thoughts. Hers were full of questions and dawning awareness. Her lips trembled. "Reid?"

Her voice broke whatever tenuous thread seemed to be holding him still. He snapped his head to the front and stepped quickly onto the bridge as if eager to be rid of his burden.

"We've got more immediate problems than lightning twenty miles away," he said, nodding toward the angry water rushing at their feet.

Again Kathryn experienced a moment of vertigo. Abandoning all pretense of dignity, she clamped her eyes shut and burrowed her head into the hair at Reid's neck. When his foot slipped once, she made a small sound of protest and clutched at him.

"Kathryn," he grunted, trying to crane his neck out of her death grip. "It's probably not a good idea to strangle your beast of burden *before* you get across the bridge."

"Oh...sorry." Immediately she loosened her hold, and they made it across without further incident. On the other side Reid let her slide onto the spongy grass verge at the side of the road.

Kathryn straightened her damp clothes, smoothed out her poncho and looked everywhere but at him.

"Thanks for all your help, Reid. I can go on alone from here. There's grass most of the way and I'll be... What's that?"

Reid glanced around, frowning. "What?"

"That noise." Kathryn started back toward the bridge, picking her way gingerly across the ground in bare feet. "It sounds like someone crying. You don't think it could be a child, do you?"

"I don't hear anything. You'd better—"

"Down there." Kathryn turned back and grasped his arm, dragging him with her. "I know I hear something!"

The safety officer by the bridge was watching them warily, and Kathryn gave him a distracted look. "Don't you hear it, officer?"

The three of them leaned over the bridge and listened for the sound Kathryn swore she had heard. Finally it came, a faint mewling.

She clutched at the arms of the men on each side of her. "It's a cat—probably just a kitten—stuck under the bridge."

Reid and the officer gazed at the sludge, debris and swirling brown water.

Slowly Reid turned his head and faced her, looking warily resigned. "And...?"

The thought of a small animal being trapped, in danger for its life, made Kathryn feel ill. She dropped her bag in the gravel and mud at her feet. Clapping both hands down on the bridge's railing, she prepared to scramble over it to the embankment. "I'm going after it!"

# CHAPTER TWO

"Oh, no you're not!" Reid hooked Kathryn around the waist and plunked her down in the muck.

She twisted out of his grasp. "But it might drown." Once again she tried to clamber over the rail, but he grabbed her again and set her firmly in the ankle-deep ooze. She swayed, grabbed at the rail and looked up at him defiantly.

"You're not going down there." His voice was firm.

"I'm not going to let it die." She thrust out her chin.

The safety officer cleared his throat. "Miss, it's probably not a good idea to risk your life to save a cat."

"But—"

"I thought you were anxious to get home," Reid said, interrupting her.

"I am—with the kitten." Her gaze never wavered. When she saw his eyes flicker, she wondered if he sensed that her earlier hurry had been to get away from him.

The officer tilted his head and looked first into Kathryn's pleading eyes, then at Reid and then down to the swirling water again. "Maybe I could go..." he began, sounding as if he would rather do anything but.

Kathryn turned to him, her face pinkening with relief. She reached out to touch his arm.

"Never mind, officer." Reid's crisp voice broke in. "I'll get the kitten. It looks like you're going to have some more business here." He pointed to the other end of the bridge where two more people were starting to cross.

The officer's quick gaze moved from Kathryn to the nervous couple holding on to the rope. He sighed. "All right, sir, but you're doing this at your own risk."

"I understand," Reid said as the officer turned away.

Kathryn beamed at him, and he lifted a quizzical brow at her as if asking what else she had expected. "I'll need something to hold on to. I'm not willing to jump in feetfirst like you." He looked back the way they had come. "There's a rope in my Jeep."

"Wait!" Kathryn dove a hand into her outsize bag and pulled out a brand-new five-foot-long leash she had bought for Bosco a few days before. "Will this do?"

Reid nodded and she handed it to him. He looped the leash over the guide rope on the bridge and hooked it onto itself. With the other end in his hand he swung over the side and prepared to descend. Just before he let himself down, he stopped and braced his feet against the steel bridge. "Kathryn, I'd appreciate it if you'd steady this as I go down," he said, indicating the rope. "I realize I'm not your favorite person, but if I'm washed away to Mexico, my mother and son might be a little upset."

Not sure how to respond, Kathryn darted forward and grabbed the rope. "If you fall, I'll be sure to send flowers," she said.

Reid gave her a swift look, and his lips twitched. "You do that." With his big hands wrapped around the leash, he let himself down one of the pilings, muttering something about women who tried to save the world.

Kathryn watched as, gingerly, he set his foot on the doghouse wedged against the bridge supports. It shifted under his weight, and Kathryn felt the leash jerk as Reid steadied himself. In slow motion he leaned down and began poking among the debris.

Chewing her lip anxiously, Kathryn entertained visions of striking rattlesnakes. She wrestled with her conscience and was about to call him back, when he bent down, moved aside a broken acacia branch and pulled up a struggling, fighting, clawing bundle of calico fur.

"Ouch. Damn!" Reid swore as, one-handed, he tried to subdue the kitten while climbing back up the side of the bridge. His ascent was much more rapid than his cautious descent, and he called out, "Get something to wrap this hellion in."

Kathryn whipped off her poncho and had it ready to encase the kitten, when Reid came up the side and thrust the spitting, hissing animal at her. With a few quick turns of her wrist she imprisoned what seemed like nine legs, three heads and five tails.

She regarded Reid warmly and blessed him with a grateful smile. "Thank you. You saved his life."

"Remind him, or her, of that on a regular basis, will you?" He paused. "You're going to keep it, aren't you?"

She beamed at him. "If I can't find his owners."

The two of them were brought spinning around when the sound of clapping started behind them. The safety officer and the couple who had just crossed the bridge were applauding Reid's efforts. Kathryn smiled as he ducked his head, grabbed up her dropped bag and took hold of her arm. "Let's get out of here. I'll see you home."

Argument would have been wasted, so she nodded and they started walking toward Raymond Road. Most of the way Kathryn was able to walk on the sidewalk, so she didn't bother to try cleaning off her feet to put on her shoes. She couldn't have done it while juggling the cat, anyway.

She glanced past the struggling bundle in her arms to view Reid's scratched and bloody hands, clucking her tongue in sympathy. "You'll have to come in when we get to my home. We've got to put some antiseptic on those scratches."

"That isn't necessary."

"But they'll get infected."

"Not in the length of time it'll take me to get home."

"But you have no idea where this kitten has been," she protested, indicating the animal with a thrust of her chin. "It might have picked up any kind of bacteria."

Reid looked at her, and she displayed her most appalled expression, the one that indicated she was prepared to go on arguing for a long time. "All right," he said.

As they walked, Kathryn speculated on why Reid was going to so much trouble for her. They had hardly spoken before yesterday—not that she hadn't tried to befriend him, she thought, feeling a little miffed. At work he seemed distant and even cold to her, but now...well, she just didn't know what to make of him.

She couldn't come to any satisfactory conclusion except that maybe he felt sorry for her or remorseful.

Kathryn sneaked a peek at his iron jaw. Fat chance! she thought.

Within twenty minutes, they had covered the four blocks to Raymond Road. She pointed out her home, a rambling structure that she knew had been built fifty years ago by an Easterner who'd come west hoping to cure a lung ailment. The walls were of desert rock and the windows were huge so sun and fresh air could pour in. They entered the gate and hurried up the walk. On the front porch they stood for a minute to catch their breath.

A large carton was sitting nearby. It was the perfect place for the kitten, Kathryn decided, as she pulled an old afghan off a lawn chair, tossed it into the carton and held the poncho over the top. A few gentle shakes tumbled the kitten into the box. It arched its back, hissed and turned in circles, looking for a way out.

Knowing the kitten would settle down after she brought it some milk, Kathryn began scraping mud from her feet onto the mat. Reid did the same, and they approached the front door, where she hesitated, peering through the door panes cautiously.

"Looking for something?" Reid's voice rumbled from behind her shoulder.

She jerked around and gave him an embarrassed half smile. "Bosco. He's been acting strange lately. Because of the storms, you know."

"So you said. Have you considered a dog psychologist?"

"I thought about it, but it's too expensive," Kathryn said, chewing her lip in indecision. Then she sighed. "I hate to ask you to do this."

He gave her a long-suffering look. "You haven't hesitated to ask me to do anything all afternoon."

"That's not true." Indignation drew her chin up. "It was *your* idea to bring me home, and for you to get the kitten. Now that we're here, there's only one thing to do. You'll have to hold my hand."

"Hold your hand," Reid repeated in a flat voice.

"Yes, so he'll think we're friends."

"I find that possibility growing more and more remote."

Kathryn's eyes flashed with irritation. "I don't like this any better than you do—"

"Oh, all right. A man could catch pneumonia waiting around out here." He reached for her hand and laced their fingers together, and she noticed how careful he was not to touch her with any of the rapidly drying blood on the backs of his hands. "Will this do, or do I need to put my arms around you, too?"

Kathryn couldn't answer for a moment. At the touch of his warm dry palm on hers she felt heat travel over her skin. Flustered, she fumbled the door open as she said, "There's no reason to be sarcastic."

A flash of fur shot from beneath a wing chair in the entryway. Growling low in his throat, the small Australian shepherd skidded across the dark green tile and slammed up against the edge of the door, which Reid was still holding open.

The dog yelped in pain and surprise, turned and bared his teeth at Reid who stepped back and looked prepared to leap onto the porch and slam the door.

"Bosco, don't you dare!" Kathryn released Reid's hand and jumped forward, dropping her bag and grabbing the dog by the collar. She rapped him hard across the nose. "No!"

The animal went stiff, his eyes rolled back, and he fell over on his left side, his legs extended from his body like four iron rods.

Reid's eyes widened. "What have you done to him? Is he having a seizure?"

"No...no he's not." Kathryn sawed on Bosco's collar. "Get up, Bosco." He didn't budge and her frantic mind couldn't recall the command to bring him out of his "dead dog" act.

Reid fell to his knees beside the prostrate canine. "Kathryn, we've got to help him."

"Oh, he's all right."

"How can you say that? You were willing to risk your life to rescue a stray kitten, and now you won't even help your own dog?"

"Reid, it's just an act."

His head pulled back as if he'd been struck a blow to the forehead. "An *act*?"

"Kathryn, what's going on?" A youthful lilting voice sounded from the hallway.

A second, more mature one chimed in. "Why are you so late? Did you get stuck in the flood?"

Kathryn stopped pulling at Bosco and looked up to meet Reid's puzzled gray eyes.

The sound of friendly chatter came closer.

With a start Kathryn realized the sound was coming from knee level. Oh, no, she thought, please don't let them be—

Around the corner of the entryway came two women, one young, one older, both dressed in shiny red tights and gold-threaded leotards...both walking on their hands.

The younger woman turned her head just enough to see the pair of mud-caked men's dress shoes. With a squeak of surprise she cartwheeled to her feet. "Kathryn," she gasped, blushing. "I'm so sorry. I didn't know you'd brought someone with you." She self-consciously smoothed her hair back and patted the dark brown braid that snaked to her waist.

The other woman also got to her feet, although more slowly as befit her seventy years. She didn't look a bit embarrassed but viewed the visitor with lively interest.

Kathryn gave them a feeble smile. "This is my boss, Reid Darwin. These are my housemates, Roxanne and Wilma Tarleton."

Wilma's attention was focused on the dog. "Why is Bosco playing dead?"

Kathryn uttered an exasperated sound. "I made the mistake of saying 'don't you dare' and he went into his routine. Now I can't remember the command to get him out of it."

Wilma snapped her fingers and said, "Wake up, Bosco."

Immediately the dog rolled to his feet and stood looking up at Kathryn, wagging his tail as if expecting a treat. When he received nothing but frowning disapproval, his head and tail drooped and he slunk under his favorite chair.

"Thanks, Wilma," Kathryn sighed in relief. Then she followed Roxie's gaze as it traveled over Kathryn's muddy feet and damp, wrinkled dress and took in Reid's stained shoes. Kathryn saw that his suit pants had mud streaks along each thigh where her feet had hung.

With her characteristic bluntness, Roxie said, "You two look like something the cat dragged in!"

"No," Reid answered with a grimace. "We dragged a cat in."

"What?"

"I'll explain later," Kathryn said hastily. She turned to Reid. "Thank you for bringing me home."

Wilma cleared her throat, her bright brown eyes going from Kathryn to the tall man behind her. "So you're Kathryn's boss, hmm?"

Kathryn thought Reid looked a bit dazed, as he slanted her a puzzled glance and said, "Yes, I am."

"Well, I hope you gave Kathryn that executive secretary's job. She deserves it—and at a considerable raise from her previous salary, I might add."

"Grandma!"

"Wilma!" Kathryn seconded Roxie's outrage.

The older woman flipped her hand impatiently.

Reid's face was beginning to lose its stunned look. "She's got the job, but she'll have to earn the raise," he said, then tilted his head. "Now you tell me, why on earth were you walking through the house on your hands?"

Wilma's thin white eyebrows shot up. "We were practicing, of course."

"Practicing?" His eyes went from her to Roxie to Kathryn.

She stretched her lips into a smile and burst into explanations. "Wilma and Roxie used to be acrobats in the circus."

"We were practicing because we're going to perform at a party this afternoon," Roxie supplied.

"Kathryn is going to be there, too," Wilma added.

Kathryn groaned and slapped a grubby hand to her forehead, leaving a muddy streak on her fair skin.

"Oh, no. I forgot!" So much for well-laid plans, she thought.

Reid looked Kathryn up and down, his expression incredulous. "You're an acrobat?"

"No, no," she said impatiently. "I'm—"

Roxie interrupted. "Come on, Kath, you've got to get ready. I'll run you some bathwater, but hurry, okay? They're counting on us." She grabbed her grandmother and they headed down the hall, this time on foot, Kathryn noted gratefully. Within seconds she could hear water roaring into the tub. It sounded heavenly compared to the noise of the pounding rain she had been hearing all afternoon.

"Who's counting on you?" Reid asked.

Distracted, Kathryn answered, "It's a birthday party..." and realized she had made a mistake when his eyes widened and his expression hovered between astonishment and horror.

Kathryn was sure he was remembering the salsa dancing incident and wondering why it had been so all-fired important for her to rush through a flood for a party. She could remind him that she had forgotten all about it, but he should be able to think of that himself. She didn't want to go into lengthy explanations, which he probably wouldn't want to hear, anyway, so she propped up her bright smile and said, "Well, thank you for all you've done," in a tone pitched to hurry him on his way. Guiltily she recalled insisting that she clean his scratches. He didn't want her fussing over them, anyway, and she was anxious to get him out the door.

He was still gazing toward the hall where Roxie and Wilma had disappeared. Slowly he focused on Kathryn's fixed smile. "Acrobats, huh? And a dog that plays dead."

"That's right. Roxie and I have been friends since high school. We used to sling burgers together. Until a few months ago, she and Wilma worked in a circus. It closed, and I invited them to live here because my parents have moved to Springerville." She took a step toward the door, eager to usher him out. She knew she was being rude, that he probably deserved more explanation, but she hoped he'd be satisfied.

Reid shook his head but couldn't seem to keep himself from asking the next question. "And Bosco?"

"He was a gift. As I said, he couldn't stand the noise of the cannon the clowns used in their act, so—"

"So he was put out of a job."

"Yes." She stared thoughtfully at Bosco. "Also, he can't seem to tell the difference between 'don't you dare' and 'drop dead.' Maybe his hearing is going." Kathryn shrugged. "Of course, he did bite the ringmaster once...."

Reid looked toward the chair from which a low, whining sound was coming. "I would have fired him, too. Good night, Kathryn. It's been an...adventure." He strode out the door and closed it firmly behind him.

Kathryn slumped gratefully against it.

Bosco slunk from beneath the chair and beseeched her with soulful brown eyes.

"It's not your fault, boy," Kathryn said, leaning over to pat his head. "I know you were scared, but did you have to try and bite my new boss?"

Bosco snuffled sympathetically against her hand as Roxie bustled up, words pouring out of her like bursts of machine gun fire. "Is he gone? Good! You've got fifteen minutes to bathe and thirty to get into costume. Why are you dawdling?"

"Because I'm exhausted."

Roxie shook her head and clucked her tongue. "A bit peevish today, are we?" While Kathryn sputtered, her roommate continued, "You'll have to be exhausted later. People are counting on you!"

Groaning, Kathryn pushed away from the door. "Do you have any idea what kind of day I've had? What kind of *two* days?"

She felt as if she was caught between two locomotives, as Wilma joined Roxie in hurrying Kathryn along.

"You can yell through the bathroom door and tell us all about it," Wilma chirped. "I'll get out your costume."

They hustled her inside and shut the door.

"A fine thing," Kathryn muttered. "Railroaded in my own home." She started to peel off her dress, then remembered the kitten. She did yell then, to tell the news to Roxie, who squealed with delight and could be heard hurrying to the front porch.

Laughing ruefully, Kathryn pulled her hair into a twist on top of her head, though she wasn't sure why she bothered. It couldn't get any more wet. She sank into the tub of hot water and fragrant bubbles, grateful that the flood hadn't affected the water system. With a sigh of pure pleasure she leaned back and closed her eyes, letting the day's traumas melt away.

Though she had told herself not to think about it, once again her mind replayed the previous day's scene with Reid, ending with his matter-of-fact statement that she would be watched very carefully and subjected to a thirty-day performance review. Kathryn kept her eyes closed, but her lips pulled down at the corners. This wasn't the first time her professionalism had been questioned.

She wondered what Reid would have said if Roxie hadn't interrupted. Kathryn had been about to tell him of her part in this evening's festivities. She could just imagine his face if she had told him the party, which was being held at a nearby rest home, was for a ninety-year-old circus fan, who had seen her perform once as her alter ego—Katydid the Clown.

Grinning wickedly at the thought of Reid's disapproval, she picked up a bath sponge and sent water cascading over her arm.

Roxie and Wilma hadn't been the only ones put out of a job by the circus closing. Kathryn had been left unemployed, too.

While Kathryn and Roxie had slapped Big Macs together and scooped up French fries after school during their junior year in high school, Roxie had related glowing accounts of her grandmother's glamorous life with the circus. After graduation, Roxie had gone to join her grandmother and hone her natural skills as an acrobat. Kathryn had gone to clown college before joining her friend.

Kathryn's eyes grew dark with the reminiscence. Those had been wonderful years. To a girl who had spent her entire life in the Sonora desert, the traveling had been a revelation. Everything about the circus had been exciting...the crowds, the performances, the other clowns who had gladly shared their knowledge with an eager newcomer. She had loved the noise and excitement, especially the roustabouts shoving and cursing the props and platforms into position. Even the breathless wait just before she made her rolling, tumbling, bumbling entrance had held its own special thrill.

Kathryn enjoyed making people happy. It was a residue of her uncertain childhood. Although her parents had seemed to have a solid marriage, they had gone through a long period of strife when she was small, which gave the impression they were headed for divorce. Kathryn, a sensitive child, had thought the problems were somehow her fault, and she'd been desperate for them to be one happy family again. She spent many a night crying herself to sleep, worrying about the future. Her parents eventually reconciled, but Kathryn was left with the desire to see people content. Clowning had provided a happy outlet for this need in her, but that career had lasted only five years.

Although rumors had been rampant that last season, it had still been a shock when the owner called everyone together and told them the circus was bankrupt.

Kathryn had stood, holding hands with Roxie and Wilma, crying over the end of a dream.

In the mad scramble for jobs in other circuses Kathryn had lost out. Clowns with more experience, better tricks, better skills had been hired before her application was even considered. To her amazement she had also run up against prejudice because she was a woman. Women clowns simply weren't as popular in the bigger circuses.

Disappointed but not discouraged, she had decided to return home. In Tucson's booming economy there would surely be enough birthday parties and company picnics to support her, she'd reasoned. She couldn't have been more wrong. Again, people who were more experienced and had been around longer got the steady work.

So she'd dusted off her typing and shorthand skills and gone job hunting. Jill Clevenger had given her a good job with a pretty good salary when no one else would, and Kathryn's gratitude was boundless. She still performed as a clown occasionally on weekends, and her clientele was growing. In fact, Jill had arranged for her to appear at the upcoming company picnic.

Kathryn sat up suddenly, almost sending water onto the floor in a fragrant tidal wave.

Darn it, she thought, slapping down the sponge. Although she missed the circus, she knew she would love her new job, and she wasn't going to be denied another job because of prejudices and misconceptions. She'd been forced to give up one career, and she certainly wasn't going to do it again.

She finished washing quickly and surged to her feet. Grabbing a towel, she wielded it in sharp quick pats over her body. It didn't matter if Reid didn't like her. She was going to prove him wrong!

THE NEXT DAY wasn't as bad as Kathryn thought it would be. She caught a ride to work with Roxie, who was on her way to yet another job interview.

The warehouse foreman at TJS checked her car and discovered a loose wire. He reconnected it and the old Buick started immediately.

Kathryn shook her head at the workings of fate, but she decided that yesterday was in the past. Her ruined dress and the new resident on her front porch served to remind her of all that had happened, but she wasn't going to dwell on it. She was determined to be professional toward Reid Darwin and try to eradicate the memory of the previous day's disasters.

On her way back into the building one of the sales reps caught up with her and held the door.

"Good morning, Jerry," she greeted him, linking her arm in his to stride down the hall. She liked him because he was sweet and grandfatherly and he told wonderful jokes.

"Mornin'," he answered, grinning. His face was wide and florid, with a mouth that turned up and brought the folds of his skin into play, creating smile upon smile. He was a top salesman, largely because he made people feel so welcome. "I hear you're taking over for Jill for a few months."

Automatically, her gaze flew ahead to Reid's office doorway. "Yes, and I hope I can handle it."

Jerry pulled his beefy arm free from hers and swung it around her shoulders to give her a squeeze. "You'll do great," he assured her, then launched into a joke as he swept her into her office.

Watching him tell a joke was often more fun than the story itself. Jerry's malleable face and rotund body stretched, exaggerated and crumpled into whatever position he needed for emphasis. By the time he finished a joke, he was usually laughing so hard he could barely get out the punch line, and so was his audience. This time was no exception, and Kathryn was using her fingertips to wipe tears of laughter from her eyes by the time he finished.

He gave her a hug as he was leaving. Kathryn had her head down, reaching for a tissue to wipe her eyes when she heard Jerry say, "Good morning, Reid."

Kathryn's head bobbed up just as Reid stepped into her doorway. Her thoughts skittered off in all directions as she noticed how cool and crisp he looked in his pin-striped suit. She thought of yesterday's happenings, then took a mental inventory of her own appearance. She gave herself points for her cream linen suit and French-rolled hair, but deducted a few for her laughter-flushed face. Her fair skin was a weather vane of her emotions. It swept with fiery redness when she was happy, embarrassed, or angry. Right now, though, the color felt as if it was fading fast.

His eyes swept over her, ending at her face. Then he cocked his head in the direction Jerry had gone. "Did I miss playtime?"

Oh, so it's like that this morning? she thought. No longer orphans of the storm, they were back to being tough boss and inexperienced secretary.

She attempted a cool smile. "It's time for me to open your mail. How are your cat scratches today?" she asked, glancing down at the hands clenched loosely at his sides.

Reid held them out, flipping the backs over. "They're just superficial," he said absentmindedly then added, "Now, get your pad, please. I want to dictate some letters." He turned back toward his own office, and Kathryn put a hand to her throat, trying to still her erratic heartbeat. She felt like a child who'd been caught with a fist in the cookie jar, but, darn it, there was nothing wrong with enjoying some fun with her fellow employees. She grabbed her pad and a handful of pencils, squared her shoulders and followed Reid.

She watched his long legs moving in a slow easy stride. The first time she'd seen him, she had been surprised that such a big man moved so easily, like a football player who had practiced ballet—although she certainly couldn't imagine him stuffed into a pair of tights. The image brought a fleeting, impish grin to her face. He stopped at his office door, turned quickly and caught her smile. She willed the corners of her mouth to smooth out. He looked as if he wanted to say something, but TJS's general manager approached at that moment, and he and Reid began discussing a shipment of defective paper towel dispensers.

Kathryn went past them into Reid's office and sat down opposite his wide mahogany desk. She crossed her knees and balanced her steno pad on top. Steadying herself with a deep breath, she looked around and tried to decide if she felt different being a step closer to the man who ran the company. Not really, she concluded, because she was still pretty low in his estimation.

She studied the room, trying to discover exactly what kind of man he was. Hardworking, she decided. There were piles of accounts-payable files on his desk, each with its blue printed check attached, awaiting his signature once he approved the paperwork.

Neat, too. A row of pens and pencils lay atop the desk. He disdained the use of a pencil holder, because, Jill had told her, items stuck up at odd angles, caught at his shirt or jacket cuffs and got in his way.

She didn't doubt he was conscientious. Everything about the company bespoke that part of his personality. And, too, he could have gone off and left her and the kitten half-drowned yesterday.

Devoted, she thought, half listening to the conversation still going on in the hall. She knew he had taken over the company after his father's death, though he'd been but twenty-eight at the time.

Her gaze rested on a photograph behind his desk. A mischievously grinning blond boy of five or six beamed out at her. Her boss was a widower, Jill had said, and was raising his son with the help of his mother. Looking at the photo of the happy-looking little boy, Kathryn couldn't help but wonder what Reid's wife had been like, and she felt sad that her life had ended too young.

She knew from yesterday's experiences that he was strong and hesitant to show weakness or vulnerability. She had been allowed only a brief glimpse of the cat scratches on his hands this morning, but she had seen that scabs were forming, long and dark on his skin. Just superficial, huh?

Against her will she felt the phantom touch of his hands on the backs of her legs, knew again the awareness that had tremored through her when she had buried her nose into the taut skin at the back of his neck.

Kathryn frowned. She couldn't think of Reid Darwin in that way and knew he would never think of her as anything but a junior secretary and an incompetent one at that....

"Getting impatient?" Reid asked, striding into the room suddenly.

Her back went straight as a freshly sawed board, and her thoughts scattered as she answered, "Certainly not."

He looked as if he didn't believe her, but he grabbed a stack of opened mail and perched on the edge of his desk to dictate replies. Kathryn's pencil flew as he spoke, and at one point he stopped to ask, "Are you keeping up all right?"

Her arm was about to fall off, and there was a cramp running up the middle of her palm, but she would never admit it. Surreptitiously she flexed her fingers around the pencil. "Of course I am," she said.

He quirked a brow at her but plunged in again. When he was finished, he sat swinging his foot against the desk, seemingly oblivious to the faint thumping sound his heel made against the wood. Kathryn skimmed her notes to make sure she had everything she needed.

"You're going to have to hire someone, you know," he said suddenly.

Stunned, Kathryn looked down at the pad of neat shorthand notes and then up at his face. "After one *day*? You said I could have a month!" Her green eyes were flashing angry gold.

"I mean someone to help you, a temp to do your old job while you do Jill's."

Kathryn allowed her back to relax against the chair. She had dreaded asking him about bringing in an assistant for fear it would seem she couldn't handle the job, but she saw now she should have brought the matter up first. She was learning a great deal very fast in her new position. "All right. I'll take care of it right away." She gave him a direct look. "I don't want to fall behind."

With a nod, he slid off the desk and moved around to his chair. "Fine."

Recognizing the dismissive tone of his voice, Kathryn stood and headed for the door.

"Kathryn," he called out, stopping her before she reached it.

She gave him an over-the-shoulder look, her eyebrows raised in question, but turned around fully at the odd look on his face. His forehead was pleated, and Kathryn braced herself.

"What are you going to name the kitten?"

She blinked, surprised as much by the grudging tone of his voice as by his question. Maybe he did care about that little scrap of fur, after all. A smile glimmered on her lips. "Hellion," she answered.

That surprised a laugh out of him, and Kathryn watched, entranced, as the lines at the corners of his eyes crinkled and years seemed to fall away from him.

Inside, something treacherous touched her, low and soft. Suppressing it, she swung around and hurried out, still speculating on the enigma that was Reid Darwin.

THE STRAIN of keeping up both her old job and her new one began telling on her quickly in the next few days. She interviewed several temporary helpers for her old position but could find no one suitable. After one particularly disappointing interview during which she was interrupted three times, Kathryn hurried home, hoping to find some peace and quiet.

When she reached the house, she patted Bosco, scooped up Hellion—he was hers now as no one had answered the Found notice the community cable station had run for her—and followed the inviting sounds of someone rustling about in the kitchen. Roxie, she thought.

"Do I dare ask where Wilma is?" she asked, as she entered the kitchen and dropped into a chair to watch Roxie tear, slice, chop and dice everything she could find into a salad for dinner. Kathryn called the cre-

ation "kitchen sink salad" because that item seemed
to be the only thing Roxie left out.

"You can ask, but you probably won't like the answer any better than I did," Roxie said, opening a jar
of green olives and sniffing the contents. Shrugging,
she drained off the brine and threw the olives into the
heaping bowl.

Kathryn grimaced. "Just tell me if it's likely to get
her arrested."

Roxie popped an olive into her mouth and seemed
to consider how to answer. "Possibly. Grandma and
some of her friends were going down to city hall to
demand better access to city buses for the handicapped."

"Well, that sounds tame enough," Kathryn said,
frowning dubiously, her hands smoothing Hellion's
calico fur.

"But with Grandma and company, who can tell?"
Roxie added with a cheerful grin. "Do you want to eat
now or wait for her?"

"Now. I had a rough day." Kathryn set the kitten on
the floor, washed her hands and gathered utensils to
set the table. "We can save her some salad and smug-
gle it to her if she's jailed and gets put on bread and
water."

Roxie laughed. "It would serve her right." She
continued working for a few moments before sliding
Kathryn a sympathetic glance. "Old Iron Eyes up to
his usual form, huh?"

The name pulled a half laugh from Kathryn. "Iron
Eyes?"

"Fits, don't you think?"

Kathryn thought about the frequent coolness of
Reid's gaze. "Yes, it does."

Roxie shrugged. "Don't complain, though. At least you've got a boss. I can't even find a job."

"I think you're too choosy," Kathryn said with the ease of a longtime friend who was more like a sister. She waved a fork at Roxie. "What about that photographer's assistant job you tried for?"

Leveling a look at her, Roxie answered, "He wanted a lot more than an assistant."

"Oops."

They finished setting the table and ate in silence until Roxie propped her elbows on the table and asked dreamily, "Do you ever miss the circus?"

"Of course. I loved the excitement of new towns, new people to entertain." Kathryn's eyes misted. "And the kids seeing a circus for the first time—that was the best part."

Roxie tapped the tabletop and brought Kathryn back to reality with, "Not to mention the leaking tent, the costumes that were falling apart and the ten thousand times that payroll was late."

Kathryn grinned, her green eyes sparkling. "I guess the saying is true . . ."

"Which one?"

"That the 'good old days' were once 'these hard times.'"

Roxie laughed in agreement as she forked up a mouthful of greenery. She chewed thoughtfully for a while. "You know, Grandma misses the circus much more than I do. It was hard for her to watch her friends go bankrupt. She and Grandpa had been with Holley Brothers from the beginning. Now she's afraid of being put out to pasture." Roxie made a sound of distress, her pretty face puckered into a frown. "Never in my wildest dreams did I imagine becoming my grandmother's caretaker. Sometimes I wish Mom and Dad would come back from Saudi Arabia and take her off my hands. I don't know how much longer I can keep up with her!''

''She'll settle down after a while,'' Kathryn assured her in soothing tones.

''We hope.'' Roxie sat up and tossed her long brown braid over her shoulder as if throwing off her worries. ''Well, at least one of us is still in the business. You have a clowning job this weekend, don't you?''

Kathryn took a moment to examine something unrecognizable in her salad, finally decided it was a dried apricot and popped it into her mouth. ''Yes, a birthday party. I can look forward to it tomorrow while I'm stuck interviewing prospective junior secretaries. I just hope I can find one who can at least type,'' she finished wearily.

Roxie sat forward suddenly. Her fork clattered into her bowl, and she reached over to grab Kathryn's wrist. Her eyes held a dawning idea, and a smile touched her lips. ''I can type.''

''Oh, no.'' Kathryn shook her head emphatically. ''No way!''

''Why not?'' Roxie asked eagerly. ''You're looking for a helper. I'm looking for a job.''

''Your qualifications—''

''Are just fine. I took a typing test the other day at one of those employment agencies, and I typed fifty words a minute. That's pretty good,'' she said in self-congratulation. ''And you said yourself, the junior secretary doesn't need to know shorthand.''

Kathryn could come up with a dozen reasons why this was a bad idea, not the least of which was what Reid would say if she hired her roommate. The company had a policy against hiring members of the same family. Of course, that didn't apply to best friends. "Okay, maybe your skills are good, but—"

"It's a great idea." Roxie forked a load of salad into her mouth and chewed thoughtfully. "We can ride together—carpool. It would save on gas, and you won't have to worry about your car breaking down again."

"Your car's in worse shape than mine!"

Roxie waved her hand negligently. "Details, details. One of them should be running most of the time. I bet I would make a good secretary," she said dreamily. "And I would love to learn about all those computers and things you use."

Kathryn reached out and shook Roxie's shoulder. "No, Rox, it wouldn't work."

Blinking, Roxie looked at her. "Why not? I've got the skills."

"Some people are simply not office material. You've always been much happier at jobs where you meet people and—"

"You mean you don't meet people in that job?"

"Of course, but not like you think. Most of the time you'd be typing letters on the personal computer or updating the lists of prices we charge our customers or swearing at the copy machine."

"I never swear."

"You will when you meet our copy machine," Kathryn said, sighing.

Roxie pounced. "*When* I meet it? Does that mean I have the job?"

"No!"

Metal clattered against crockery as Roxie dropped her fork into her bowl and pushed them both away.

Leaning forward, she propped her forearms on the table and stared Kathryn in the eye. "Okay, what's your biggest objection?"

Kathryn studied Roxie's earnest face. Hurt was beginning to show in her friend's expression, and she shifted her gaze away, answering uncomfortably, "What Reid will say." Kathryn gave her friend a troubled glance. "If something went wrong, he would blame me."

"What could possibly go wrong?" Roxie's hands flew wide as if asking the universe to be witness to her innocence.

"Got an hour?"

Roxie rolled her eyes heavenward. "Okay, okay, so I've done a few impetuous things in my life."

"Putting the fat lady's nightgown on a baby elephant and tying him up in the ringmaster's trailer was more than impetuous," Kathryn pointed out dryly. "It's a wonder you didn't get fired."

A reminiscent smile lighting her face, Roxie answered, "Yeah, I guess. It was sure funny, though."

"Only because the fat lady was in on it with you." Kathryn paused. "I've never asked, but how did you two get that elephant through the door?"

Roxie popped another olive into her mouth and grinned. "Bacon grease." When she saw Kathryn fighting a smile, she said, "I wouldn't do anything like that at Tucson Janitorial Supplies. I promise."

"I don't know, Rox..." Kathryn hedged.

Sensing her advantage, Roxie pressed. "You're tired of interviewing people, you know I can do the job, and you're used to bossing me around, so..."

Irate, Kathryn sat up. "I don't boss you. If anything, it's the other way around."

"Then how can you pass up a golden opportunity to get back at me?"

Kathryn chewed her lip as her roommate waited expectantly. The past few months had been rough on Roxie, too. Trained as a circus performer, she had been having a hard time settling into anything else. Plus, coping with Wilma's restless energy was difficult. And Kathryn did want to see her friend content.

Across the table Roxie summoned her most winning smile. "Please."

Kathryn's hands flew into the air as she laughed. "I give up! All right. Come in first thing tomorrow and fill out an application." She shook a warning finger an inch from Roxie's pert nose. "But if you do anything to get me in trouble with Reid—"

"I'll quit right away, Kath. I promise," she said, her brown eyes earnest. "But nothing's going to go wrong."

# CHAPTER THREE

"WHAT'S YOUR ROOMMATE doing here?" Reid's voice, coming from her office doorway, pulled Kathryn around. He was staring at Roxie carrying a stack of mail to the accounting department.

Here it comes, she thought, rising to her feet. She frequently stood when he came into the room, wanting to grasp whatever bit of advantage she could, but this time when he turned and looked at her, she felt an increasingly familiar tightening at the back of her neck. She tried doubly hard to sound businesslike when she answered. "Roxie is my new assistant—until Jill comes back and I can return to my own job."

Reid moved into the room. With his eyes on her, he arranged his solid bulk in the visitor's chair opposite her desk. Having him sit down in her office was so unprecedented Kathryn just stared at him for a second before she sank into her own chair.

He turned slightly sideways, his big shoulders resting against the wall and one elbow propped on the chair back. "Your assistant? Do you think that's wise?"

Kathryn listened for the prickly impatience he often showed when questioning her. To her surprise, he sounded only curious. She wondered at his change of attitude but wasn't going to question her good luck.

Because she had been on the delivering end of the same argument with Roxie the night before, Kathryn knew just what to say. "You said I should hire someone," she pointed out reasonably. "Roxie has all the skills we need. I've worked with her before, and it's only temporary, anyway."

The bluntly carved edges of his mouth arranged themselves into a small smile. "A multimillion-dollar company is slightly different from a fast-food restaurant."

"Oh, but we worked together in—" Her mind went to the upcoming picnic and Jill's insistence on surprise for Kathryn's involvement. "Other capacities," she finished lamely, glancing down at her hands. She picked up a pen and ran her slim fingers over it. "Believe me, Roxie is qualified for this job. A temporary position such as this will help her make the transition from the circus to a new career."

Reid's glance slid over her in slow appraisal, lighting on the coppery curls escaping her barrettes and then on the surplice bodice of her jade-green dress. "Okay. You seem to be taking to Jill's job pretty well—and now that you're a supervisor, it's your decision. But remember, this is a business—my business—not a philanthropic society."

"Of course."

His intent regard caused warmth to seep over her throat and up her face. Tension curled into her, pulling her lips open. Something about him tugged at her, intrigued while it irritated. His occasional flashes of warmth and humor strummed an answering chord in her. A compliment or kind word brought a surge of joy. She didn't understand him, but she responded to him.

Slowly, imperceptibly, Reid was moving closer. She felt her expression soften, as her gaze met his. For a long pulsing moment she tried to read his changing signals—restraint, which he usually showed her, tinged by a curiosity she had never seen directed at her before, and a startling flash of desire followed by anger.

She dropped the pen, and her hand stole across the desktop toward it. "Reid? Is something wrong?"

The signals he had been sending were gone in an instant. He straightened, his face shuttered, then stood to move to the door. "Just remember, you're responsible for the quality of Roxie's work."

Kathryn's mind struggled to change direction as quickly as his did. "Yes, of—of course," she stammered. The naked and complex honesty of that one look from him had unnerved her, but she had no time to dwell on it before her new assistant sailed in.

"All done with the mail," Roxie sang out as she swept into the room. She rubbed her hands together. "Now are you going to show me the personal computer? I can't wait to learn."

Catapulted out of her troubling thoughts, Kathryn nodded, picked up a manual and prepared for Roxie's first lesson.

Roxie turned out to be an avid pupil. If she used unorthodox methods to get the computer to do what she wanted, Kathryn just closed her eyes to it. Her own workload was heavy and she was grateful that by the end of the second week, Roxie was handling things well enough.

Kathryn wasn't at all surprised to see how Roxie handled the men in the office, as well. They swarmed around her like bees in clover. While the other employees appreciated Kathryn's friendliness, Roxie's flirtatiousness was a real hit. Kathryn watched in amused wonder as one man after another, young, old, married or single, fell victim to her roommate's charm.

Even Reid wasn't immune, apparently, Kathryn discovered when she came into the small office one day after taking notes in an accounting meeting.

He was perched on a corner of Roxie's desk, laughing at something she'd said and in the moment before he turned to see who had walked in, Kathryn glimpsed genuine pleasure on his face. His gray eyes were alight, the lines that so often bracketed his mouth were smoothed out, and his blunt features were positively handsome.

Kathryn felt an unreasonable twitch of jealousy in realizing that it had been Roxie who had pleased him so.

He stood up when he spotted her, his laughing expression melting into a more formal one. "All finished in the accounting meeting? Good. I wonder if you'd call and make lunch reservations for Breck Snyder and me at Raintrees. One o'clock." He smiled and nodded at Roxie as he left.

Kathryn pursed her lips, and color washed up to ride high on her cheeks. Roxie could have flipped through the Rolodex and made the reservations while the two of them were having such a good time, she thought peevishly as she sat down and reached for her phone.

"Something wrong, Kath?"

She looked up to see real concern in Roxie's face and instantly regretted her thoughts. "No, just tired, I guess. I'm ready for the weekend."

Roxie's voice lowered to a near whisper. "You won't get much rest Saturday, because of the picnic. But Sunday you should try to sleep late."

Kathryn nodded. "I'll try." She regretted that Roxie wouldn't be at the company picnic, too, but she was a Girl Scout leader, and her troop had an overnight campout to attend.

She reached for the phone and booked her boss a table for lunch, and she smiled her way through the rest of the day, avoiding Reid as much as possible, along with her own troubled thoughts about him.

The next day Kathryn began at noon to transform herself into Katydid for the company picnic. The house was quiet with Roxie gone, and Wilma was busy painting slogans demanding better care for the elderly onto big pieces of poster board. She and some friends planned to picket city hall on Monday.

The peaceful household would make it easier to get into the personality of Katydid, Kathryn thought, as she sat down at her vanity table and got out her makeup kit. During her years with the circus she had gotten into costume with her mirror propped on makeshift tables or sometimes on the ground. She had lost her kit more than once during setup at a new town and had had to borrow from the other clowns or make do with white shoe polish, a piece of charcoal and a tube of lipstick, but she wouldn't have traded a moment of those years for anything. Happily she flipped open the blue case and dug in.

Katydid was everything Kathryn wasn't but sometimes wanted to be. Katydid could be a childlike goof-off with a little-girl voice that squeaked hilariously. Kathryn wore demure suits and dresses in colors designed not to clash with her hair; Katydid wore what she darn well pleased. Her favorite costume was a flouncy red skirt and a blouse, with a big frilly bonnet atop a frizzy yellow wig. Kathryn's clear skin needed no makeup, just a little mascara to enhance her long, pale eyelashes; Katydid looked like a little girl who had gleefully taken liberties with her mother's makeup kit.

Katydid was a bumbler who got into a great deal of trouble trying to do the simplest things.

Like all clowns developing a character, Kathryn had given much thought to what Katydid would be like. Drawing on the real failings and fears of human nature, Kathryn had made Katydid a little girl who struggled to do things well. Much to Katydid's chagrin, though, they always fell apart for her.

Her shoes constantly came untied. It had taken hours of practice for Kathryn to tie Katydid's enormous shoes tight enough to stay on but loose enough to come undone. Katydid's knee socks were always falling down—aided by a slip-knotted elastic that worked itself free every few minutes.

When Katydid did magic tricks, the audience had to help her or she couldn't get them right. When she juggled, she invariably bopped herself on the head, causing the children in the audience to laugh and scramble to her assistance.

Kathryn opened her tube of makeup, grateful that at least she wouldn't have to worry about sunburn today. Clown white was mainly composed of zinc oxide.

Spreading the thick cover cream on her fingers she began working it into her skin until not a trace of her complexion showed. Next she took a cotton swab and drew lines through the thick white greasepaint. With a black pencil she defined big circles around her eyes, filling in the space between the eye and the black line with triangles of blue and yellow. She glued big false eyelashes in place and batted them to make sure they would stay on in the day's heat.

Kathryn debated about wearing her red rubber nose. On hot days she sweated inside the rubber and occasionally had trouble breathing. She finally decided to start off wearing it and try to stay in the shade as much as possible. As the finishing touch she exaggerated her lips with red lipstick.

Satisfied, she donned a large pair of tinted glasses, the old-fashioned kind that looked like butterfly wings. Katydid wore them because she thought they looked chic. In reality they kept sliding down and getting in the way of magic tricks and juggling.

At last Kathryn pulled on her flouncy, frilly costume, yellow wig and ruffled bonnet. With each addition to her costume she grew more and more excited.

She called a goodbye to Wilma, who wished her luck, and headed for her car. Driving in costume created its own hazard, although she had long ago learned not to put on her big shoes until she reached her destination. People in nearby cars invariably spotted her and waved, and she usually had to drive one-handed so she could wave back. She sometimes wished she had a snappy convertible rather than her staid old Buick.

The park was one she had occasionally visited as a child. She was familiar with the layout and had already planned a spot for her props.

As soon as she arrived and set up under a big cottonwood tree, she was surrounded by a crowd of children and adults. It amused her to come face-to-face with people she worked with every day and have them fail to recognize her. She found herself wishing Jill could be there to savor everyone's surprise when Kathryn revealed her true identity. Jill loved surprises and had formed the plan as a joke.

Kathryn swung her hands wide to indicate her audience should sit on the grass, and let her alter ego take over.

"Hello, everybody." Katydid greeted them with such a big wave it sent her spinning in a circle. The children giggled and the adults smiled. Telling the audience how delighted she was to be there, she pulled out what looked like a green feather duster and confided to the children they were really flowers. She put them behind her back and brought them out again with a great flourish. To her intensely expressed disappointment, no flowers had appeared.

"I'll try again," she squeaked in her little-girl's voice. She pushed a lever in the handle of the feather duster as she stuck it behind her back again. The blooms appeared. Pretending to be searching for the lost bouquet, she turned her back so the children could see them, then flipped the lever again and pulled them out. No flowers. Katydid looked ready to weep.

The children began yelling, trying to tell her where to find them. Her bumbling attempts to locate the bouquet went on for several minutes.

At one point Katydid broke into the sign language she had learned from a friend, a deaf clown, to express her sorrow and frustration. Shaping both hands into the manual alphabet sign for the number five, she held them in front of her face and drew them down slowly, as if tears of sadness were flowing down her cheeks. One little boy who had been jumping and pointing with the others stopped and sat up straight, she noticed, his eyes riveted to her.

After a little more sleight of hand Katydid finally managed to see the flowers. With a big sigh and much eyelash fluttering behind her lightly tinted glasses, Katydid sniffed the colorful bouquet—just as an imaginary bee flew out and stung her on the nose. Katydid jumped, rubbing her nose, and the children roared with laughter.

By the time she had done her magic, made balloon animals for twenty children and painted their faces, Katydid was ready for a break.

When the children began to drift away, the little boy who had been watching her so intently from a dis-tance marched up. Lifting his right hand, he held it to his forehead, palm out and gave her a salute.

She recognized the sign for hello and returned the gesture.

The little boy, a darling blonde with big blue eyes, grinned, revealing a gap for two front teeth. "Do you know sign?" He questioned with his hands, and she realized that he was deaf.

"Yes," Katydid admitted, silently blessing Maxie, the deaf clown she had worked with. He had taught her sign, during their long hours on the circus train.

With a start Kathryn remembered where she had seen the boy before. His picture was on her boss's desk. He was Reid Darwin's son.

"Hello, Sean," she signed. "It's nice to meet you."

His eyes grew wide. "How did you know my name?"

She winked. "A little bird told me."

"You talk bird, too?"

"Only a peep," she said, and when he gave a husky chortling laugh, she fell instantly in love.

Sean became her shadow from that moment. He was a delightful imp—bright and trusting. He told her silly jokes, played tricks on her and insisted she paint a big black spider on his cheek. She was pleased at how smart he was. When she finger-spelled a word, he caught on instantly and could form sentences far more complex than Kathryn would have imagined him capable of.

As she worked to make the spider as hairy and scary as possible, Kathryn thought about Reid. No wonder he seemed so distant at times.... Life had dealt him some unfair blows. Of course, Jill had told her that his wife had died in a car wreck two years before, but Kathryn had had no idea the child Reid was raising possessed such special needs.

Kathryn might have felt pity for Sean if she hadn't worked with Maxie for five years. He was a superb clown and a wonderful person. Because of him she knew it was possible to have a rewarding career, a sense of humor and zest for life in spite of deafness.

She tried to imagine what kind of father Reid was—and formed a picture of his gentle compassion when Jill was in pain. She couldn't guess, though, whether or not having a child with a handicap would be a blow to his pride. After all, how well did she know Reid?

She was just finishing painting Sean's face when a large shadow fell over the two of them. Sean looked up, and a familiar voice said, "Sean, you'd better let her have a break."

Sean grinned and launched himself at his father.

Kathryn rose from the small folding stool she had been using to put herself on the little boy's level and busied herself packing away the paints. Apprehension quivered in her as she turned slowly to face her boss.

"She painted this big, mean spider on me." Sean signed so fast his fingers almost tangled.

Here it comes, Kathryn thought. He won't like it.

When her eyes completed the long journey up to his face, she was jolted. He was smiling, looking happier and more relaxed than he had ever been with her. In fact, he was dressed more casually than she had ever seen him before, in faded jeans and a cotton knit shirt.

He held out his hand. "Sean tells me you speak his language. That's great. Few people do."

Kathryn lifted her hand slowly, momentarily speechless. The second shock came when her fingers touched his. He grasped them warmly, his smile brightening by several degrees, his gray eyes deepening to a smoky hue. She didn't know what to think. Except for the unusual circumstance of being caught in a flood together, he had never been this friendly to her.

Her face felt suddenly hot, and she was glad for the makeup that disguised her betraying blush. Of course, how could she have forgotten? He didn't recognize her. He didn't have a clue who she really was.

"It's nice to meet you," he went on. "I'm Reid Darwin." He considerately signed as he spoke so Sean wouldn't be left out of the conversation.

"She knows," the little boy said, tapping Reid's arm to gain his attention. "A bird told her."

Reid laughed and glanced back at Katydid.

She had paused so long in saying anything he was beginning to look at her strangely. Kathryn opened her mouth to speak then thought better of it. She didn't want him to recognize her voice—not quite yet, anyway. The sensation of basking in his approval was too pleasant and heady to give up.

She spoke in Katydid's high-pitched, little-girl voice, while signing for Sean. "Learning sign can be a bit tedious. Besides, most people don't know anyone who's deaf, so they don't have to learn it."

"That's true." He looked down at the artwork decorating his son's cheek. "This looks great." He knelt to be on Sean's level. "You're pretty scary."

Sean wiggled with pleasure. "Yeah, I'm a mean guy."

Reid laughed again, a low satisfying rumble that brought Kathryn a sharp stab of intense pleasure. "Well, mean guy, why don't you go play on the swings for a little while and let the clown—"

"Katydid," Sean interrupted, spelling the name with his fingers, then pointing to the big wooden trunk Kathryn carried her magic props in to indicate where he had learned her name.

"Katydid, then," Reid corrected himself. "Let her have a break."

Sean's lips pulled down in a pout, making his painted spider droop comically. Reid fought a smile at his son's forlorn face.

"I don't want—"

Reid slipped his hand firmly under Sean's chin. He looked directly into his eyes and signed, "Please be considerate of other people. Katydid needs a break, and it's good for you to play with the other kids."

Kathryn was impressed by how gently but firmly Reid dealt with his son. For Sean's benefit she stretched her arms out wide and faked a big yawn. "I'm so tired from doing all that magic, Sean. I do need to rest for a while. Why don't you play a little bit, then I'll show you how to juggle, okay?"

Sean's face brightened and he gave an endearing squeak of pleasure. He punched the air with one fist in a little-boy sign of triumph, turned and darted toward the swing sets.

"You don't have to do that," Reid said, straightening his big body to its full height. "It isn't necessary to give all your time to one kid."

"I'm not," she answered quickly, still using Katydid's voice. "Once I start showing him how to juggle, I'll have the whole bunch of them back here for a lesson."

Reid looked as if he wanted to continue the conversation, but Kathryn was reluctant. The more time she spent around him, the more likely it was that he would discover who she really was. Besides, she had to be by herself for a while to think about this unexpected new side to her boss.

"Well, I think I'll go over to the food tent." She pointed across the lawn to where an awning was stretched between supporting poles and huge containers of sodas were on ice. "I need something to drink."

"Great idea."

Reid was about to fall into step beside her when someone called him to join a softball game. To Kathryn's amazement he gave her a regretful look and a wink just before he loped off.

She stared after him. Where had he been hiding this other personality? And why? She was pierced by a quick stab of resentment. He seemed to like Katydid. Why didn't he like Kathryn Evans?

She crossed her arms and stood for a moment running her fingers around the flounced and ruffled hem of her sleeve. Although she knew she should let him know Katydid's identity, Kathryn hesitated. It was so rare for her to see this joking, playing, even loving, side of him. If she told him she was Kathryn he would probably nod politely, smile and avoid her for the rest of the day.

Her gaze strayed to where Reid was playing baseball with some of the other adults. He'd just slid into home plate, and when the umpire called him safe he'd jumped high in the air. On the other hand, she could go ahead as planned and reveal her identity at the end of the day. It would be a great story to cheer up Jill—and Kathryn could see more of Reid's pleasant side.

That decided, she grinned in anticipation and swung off toward the food tent.

# CHAPTER FOUR

TRUE TO HIS PROMISE, Sean let her have a half hour of rest before he showed up with his impish, gap-toothed grin and a request that she teach him how to juggle. Kathryn couldn't resist sweeping him into a hug. With his funny little laugh he wiggled away and made a dive for her box of props. She gave him a ball and showed him how to toss it from one hand to the other.

He stood with his feet wide apart, in a stance that reminded her of his father, and concentrated on keeping the ball moving between his hands. Kathryn bit her lip in amusement at the way he held his mouth...just so. When he had mastered one ball, Kathryn rewarded him with another hug, which he accepted with eye-rolling patience. She gave him a second ball and he worked earnestly to keep them both in the air at once.

As she had anticipated, the rest of the children hurried over to join them. In no time at all she had twenty children juggling. Balls flew everywhere.

The art of juggling was much harder than it looked and after a few frustrating tries, most of the children dropped their balls back into the prop box and wandered off. A few of the bigger children—and Sean—kept working. Kathryn smiled at how like his father he was—persistent.

"It looks like they're having fun," a voice said from behind her. "You really have a way with children."

Kathryn straightened from picking up the scattered props. A woman with icy white hair and a warm smile was now standing beside her. She was dressed in an elegant red jumpsuit and wore thick gold chains at her throat.

"I just have to keep them all interested," Kathryn squeaked out in Katydid's voice, trying to decide which employee this woman was related to.

"True juggling, indeed."

Sean ran over to them and tugged on the woman's sleeve. He laid the juggling balls carefully between his sneakered feet and signed, "Watch me, Grandma. I can do it better than anybody."

Laughing at his boast the woman gave him all her attention, while Kathryn studied her. So, she thought, this was Reid's mother. Their eyes were the same clear gray, but otherwise he didn't look a bit like her.

She drew her eyes back to Sean, who, to her amazement, was actually juggling three balls—a startling accomplishment for a six-year-old.

Not wanting to distract him, she waited until he had finished before signing, "That's wonderful. You're the best juggling student I ever had! You deserve a reward."

Sean dropped the balls at his feet and gave her a wearily resigned look. "Not another hug."

Mrs. Darwin and Kathryn both burst out laughing at his aggrieved expression.

"No, a different kind of reward." Kathryn went to her prop box and pulled out a tiny flashlight. No bigger than a ballpoint pen, it gave off a strong beam of light when switched on. She shopped at bargain stores to pick up fun prizes to hand out whenever she had a clowning job.

When she presented the flashlight to Sean, his eyes got huge with delighted wonder. He chortled deep in his throat and accepted the gift. This time, *he* gave the hug, throwing his arms around Kathryn's waist and squeezing hard. He touched his fingers to his lips, then extended them outward, palms up. "Thank you, thank you."

Just as the softball game was finishing, he ran to show the prize to his father. Reid tossed his glove to another player and swung his son up into his arms.

Kathryn gasped when Reid carelessly turned his little boy upside down, bent over, placed Sean's legs around his neck and stood up in one powerful movement. He settled Sean on his shoulders as he walked over to join Kathryn and Mrs. Darwin.

"Don't be alarmed, my dear," the older woman said. "He's never dropped the boy—yet."

Kathryn smiled nervously.

Striding up to them, Reid said, "I hope you realize, Katydid, that now you've got a willing slave for life."

"I can't think of any slave I'd rather have than Sean," she signed, winning a puzzled look from Sean.

"What's a slave?" Sean asked.

Reid looked pained. "I've got to remember not to use phrases I don't feel like explaining to him." He set Sean back on his feet and went into a long explanation.

Kathryn wanted to watch—she was so fascinated by Reid's patience—but Mrs. Darwin was speaking to her.

"Won't you join us for something to eat?"

Kathryn looked around at her scattered things. "Well, I don't know..." she said. It *was* what she wanted, but maybe she shouldn't be too pushy.

"Please join us," Reid added, looking up. "Sean and I would like you to. Besides, my team won the game. I feel like celebrating." His face was flushed and perspiring and his hair was lying in damp, mussed waves over his forehead. As she watched he lifted his arm and blotted his face on his shirtsleeve, then put his hands on his hips and waited for her answer. His breathing was shallow and rapid, his grin boyishly eager. He was the very essence of approachable, desirable masculinity.

Something in her trembled and turned to reckless desire. She had to resist the urge to reach up and push his hair out of his face. Her palm itched to run along his jaw and cup his square chin.

She beamed at him. "I'd like that. I'd like that very much."

Reid gave her a sharp, fleetingly puzzled glance, then smiled. "Good." Sean bounced as he walked beside his father and indicated his joy by switching his flashlight on and off several times.

As they walked, Mrs. Darwin looked around. "Reid, isn't your new secretary here today? I wanted to meet her."

"Oh!" Jolted, Kathryn stumbled over her outsize shoes, and Reid's hand shot out to wrap around her arm, steadying her.

"Hey," his voice rumbled in concern. "Are you all right?"

"Yes," she said, not needing to fake the squeak. "It's just these silly shoelaces." She bent quickly to retie her shoes, keeping her head down. Good grief, why hadn't she thought of that? Of course someone would ask where she was.

She could feel Reid's eyes watching her as he answered his mother. "You mean Kathryn Evans? I don't know."

Mrs. Darwin's silver brows rose just a bit. "She did plan to come, didn't she?"

"I assumed she would."

The coolness in his voice was unmistakable, and Mrs. Darwin picked up on it. She studied him for a moment, her brow wrinkled with concern. "Oh, well, I guess you've been so busy with other things since Jill left that the subject never came up," she said, offering him an excuse.

"Yeah, I guess so."

Kathryn experienced a flurry of irritation with him. He just hadn't wanted to know if she was coming—or anything else personal about her. She stretched out the shoe-tying as long as possible, to give herself time to control her feelings, but she finally had to stand up again.

Reid smiled at her and she said, "Let's go." Her decision not to be angry was swift and sure.

The crowd around the refreshment tent was finally beginning to thin, but there was plenty of food.

They filled their plates with barbecued ribs, roasted corn and potato salad, then found a spot under a tree to eat. Kathryn's wig and bonnet were becoming unbearably hot and cumbersome, but she didn't dare take off more than the bonnet, knowing her hair would give her away.

As they ate, Reid and his mother talked about the company, and Kathryn listened with interest to his observations. Clearly, he loved the company and, even after six years, still missed his father's advice and guidance.

To her pleasure Kathryn learned a few other things about him, too. He could really pack away the food, she noted, amused when he tucked into his third helping. He ate with gusto, encouraging Sean to do the same. Also, she found out he was an avid baseball fan. Since she knew something about the game, they compared players and scores, quoted batting averages and pitching records.

Kathryn found it all immensely pleasant.

By the time the four of them had finished eating, it was beginning to grow dark. Kathryn immediately felt better at the drop in temperature and considered doing a second magic show for the children. Many of their balloon animals had popped, and she thought it would be a nice gesture to replace them, if she could muster up the energy.

She let her eyes drift a few feet over to where Reid was half dozing against the base of a cottonwood tree. Mrs. Darwin had wandered off to visit some of the other women. Sean had finished his food, and his face was liberally decorated with mustard and ketchup. He was busy inspecting the insides of his father's ears with his new flashlight.

Kathryn watched Sean for a few minutes as he pulled and tugged at Reid's ears. He reminded her of a puppy happily mauling its parent. She reached over and tapped him on the shoulder. "What are you looking for?"

"Cooties," he spelled out solemnly.

She fell back laughing.

One of Reid's gray eyes opened, and Kathryn gulped into silence, fearing he would recognize her laugh.

"What's going on...?" Reid's voice, low and rumbling, slurred just a little with sleep, spread a pleasant glow through her.

"Sean is looking for cooties," she signed.

He chuckled and reached up one big hand to tweak his son's ear affectionately. The little boy giggled and ducked but didn't give up his quest.

Reid's gaze traveled over her. She was propped on one elbow, her flounced skirt spread around her, a large expanse of slim leg showing from beneath its ruffled hem. Lazily, he inspected her slim waist and the fullness of her breasts beneath the frilly blouse. One corner of his mouth drew up slowly, crinkling into interesting lines.

A warm, sweet feeling diffused through Kathryn like honey through a sieve when he silently mouthed Katydid. He had a faintly surprised look in his eyes as if he had just rediscovered something pleasant but long forgotten.

Never had he looked more attractive to her, Kathryn thought. For a moment she thought he might feel the same about her, if his interested gaze was any indication.

Oh, of course, she jeered at herself. He was obviously turned on by white greasepaint and yellow hair. Still, she couldn't help being thrilled at the moment of closeness between them.

After a while Reid's eyes closed, the smile still curving his lips. Kathryn got up and tiptoed away, leaving Sean to ensure his father's health against creepy-crawlies.

She gathered a group of children and began teaching them magic tricks. It soon became too dark to see the props, so Kathryn dismissed the children and collected her things. Reid came up to her as she was returning from putting her prop box in her car.

"Getting ready to go, huh? Need help carrying things to your car?"

Kathryn took off the tinted glasses that were making it even more difficult to see in the gathering dusk. "Thanks, but I'm almost done."

He nodded and looked around, a slight frown indenting his forehead. "Where's Sean?"

She followed the direction of his sweeping gaze. "He hasn't been over here. The last time I saw him, he was inspecting your ears with his flashlight."

"I guess I dozed off, and when I woke up, he was gone. I thought he was with you." Alarm sprinted across Reid's face and he spun away. "I've got to find him."

Frightened, Kathryn ran after him. Her trick shoelace came untied again and, clicking her tongue in exasperation, she stopped to fix it. By the time she caught up with Reid, he had organized several men to help search. At any other time she would have found it humorous to see the company vice presidents running around so frantically.

"Where can I look?" she asked Reid.

"In the parking lot," he said, barely sparing her a glance. "I'm headed that way myself."

The lot was still crowded with cars, and one was pulling out of its slot just as Reid and Kathryn crested the small rise behind the lot. As it started forward, Sean darted out from between two parked vehicles.

"Sean!" The two adults shouted together and dashed down the hill.

The driver blared his horn and the car rocked to a stop. Sean, reacting to the car's headlights and the sudden movement, threw his arms over his head and shrieked.

Reid rushed over and swept the boy into his arms, his voice shaking as he whispered, "Dear God, Sean, what got into you?"

The driver, a teenage boy, opened his door and stood up. Even in the yellowish glow of the parking lot lights, the young man looked ashen. "Is he all right?"

Reid couldn't seem to answer, so Kathryn did. "Yes, he's all right. Just scared."

In a burst of fright-induced anger, the driver said, "Yeah, me, too. Why don't you watch your kid better?" He slammed his door and drove off.

Reid had given her a startled glance when she spoke, but he turned toward the streetlight so Sean could see his hands. "Where have you been?"

Sean blinked and pointed to the pavement. "Right here."

"I thought you were with the other kids doing magic with Katydid. She thought you were with me."

"I was with myself."

Reid closed his eyes and looked as if he was praying for patience.

Kathryn touched the little boy's arm. "Why did you wander off?"

"I saw you coming this way. I followed you, but then it was dark, and I didn't know which way to go. I couldn't see you."

Weak with relief at the child's narrow escape, Kathryn patted his back. "Next time use your flashlight to find the way."

He nodded, his bottom lip trembling as he realized he had done wrong, and buried his face against his father's neck.

Reid gave her a sharp look as his arms closed tightly around his son. "Let's take him back to my mother—" he paused before adding "—Kathryn."

She started when it dawned on her that she had been speaking in her regular voice for the past several minutes. She stared after him as his long legs strode up the hill, then she hurried along behind, having sensed from his hard tone that the picnic was over in more ways than one.

Mrs. Darwin was still frantically searching the playground when they arrived. Reid set his son on the ground, and she rushed over to hug Sean, her fingers jerking as she scolded him for disappearing. The other searchers came back, relieved that the little boy had been found unharmed.

Sean hid, his blond head tucked against his father's thigh, looking frightened by all the commotion he had caused. Mrs. Darwin pried him away from Reid and led him to the car.

"What happened? Where was he?" The question came from the company's receptionist, who had hurried up to stand beside Kathryn.

"He followed me to the parking lot and got too close to a moving car," Kathryn explained.

"That's too bad, but at least he's all right."

"Yes, he's fine."

Ginny gasped, then her eyes widened. "Kathryn Evans? Is that you?"

Heads turned in their direction, and Kathryn's eyes darted to Reid when she answered, "Yes, I'm afraid it is."

"My gosh, I didn't know you were a clown," Ginny crowed, standing back to get a better look at the Katydid costume. "I wondered where you were today. And you were here all along. Well, aren't you the sneaky one."

Kathryn heard Reid mutter, "I'll say," just before several more people began to congratulate her on her great performance. When they questioned her, she told about her years in the circus. Her explanation about Jill's insistence on surprise had them nodding their heads affectionately as they all acknowledged her love for surprises—all except Reid, who stood apart and watched her through narrowed eyes.

Laughing and offering still more congratulations, the crowd began to disperse. Reid thanked each person for coming and for helping to look for Sean.

When Kathryn started to slip away, he stopped her. "Wait a minute. I want to talk to you."

She turned, wary of his tone. "Oh? About what?"

He stood directly in front of her in an aggressive stance, feet wide apart and hands on hips. "How long have you been planning this?"

Kathryn's makeup-coated brows drew together in puzzlement. She held out her skirt. "You mean clowning? Since the day I started work at your company. Jill saw my past jobs on my résumé and thought clowning incognito would make a great surprise for today's picnic."

"More than six months ago."

She nodded slowly, her eyes never leaving him as she tried to decipher his tone and expression. "That's right."

"Why didn't you tell me?"

"Why? It was just part of the day's entertainment—it's no big deal." Her eyes widened in sudden understanding. "Oh! I'll bet you're telling yourself that I'm just as frivolous and flighty as you thought. It's bad enough having me work for you, isn't it? Finding out I'm a clown is just too much!"

Reid dropped his hands to his sides, briefly knotted them into fists, then relaxed them. "Don't be ridiculous. I don't think that. I was surprised.... You're right, it's no big deal." He turned to the parking lot. "Come on. I'll see you to your car."

A swift upward glance at his face told Kathryn that he was perfectly calm and pleasant, but she couldn't shake the feeling that his expression and words weren't true mirrors of his thoughts.

She wasn't sure why he was angry, but she knew she certainly wasn't guiltless, either. Earlier she had considered telling him who she was and had decided against it. Her motives had been selfish—she had wanted to get to know him better. She wasn't sure if that had been accomplished, or if it had been worth the effort. Today had been a mistake, she thought sadly. It would have been better if she had kept her clown act away from TJS.

Kathryn carried her troubled thoughts with her as Reid escorted her to her car, said good-night and strode away. Kathryn watched in the rearview mirror as she started the engine, but he didn't glance back.

Reversing out of the parking slot, she headed out of the park and drove home. The discomfort that had been threatening due to the weight of her wig and the day's heat was developing into a full-fledged headache. Along with it, her stomach felt as if it was in a permanent double knot.

She spent an uncomfortable night and woke up exhausted on Sunday morning. She dressed in a short cotton romper and wandered out of her room, rubbing her eyes.

Because it was early in the day, Roxie, who had returned from her Girl Scout campout, pulled a chaise lounge under the tallest of the orange trees. She made Kathryn lie on it, then clucking sympathetically, she brought her a pitcher of lemonade and insisted that she rest.

That turned out to be easier said than done, Kathryn discovered. Her mind kept replaying the scene with Reid, and she squirmed, flopping onto her back and throwing an arm up to shield her eyes from the bright day. Finally she gave up trying to sleep and called for Roxie to come and keep her company.

After discussing the situation with Roxie, it occurred to Kathryn that Reid's anger might have been self-directed since, for once, he had let down his guard and exposed his human side to her.

She had thought his feelings for her were prompted by simple dislike, but now she wondered. His reaction had been out of proportion, as if he was punishing himself for letting her get close.

Kathryn sat up, poured herself another glass of lemonade and stared into the orange tree's dark green leaves. One slim fingertip made tracks in the condensation on the outside of her glass. Two cleared trails joined into one and a fat drop of moisture ran down into her palm. With damp fingers she rubbed at the dull ache in her temple.

For a short time at the picnic she had basked in Reid's friendship and approval, only to have it snatched away. His actions hurt her, and it took a lot of thought to sift through the reasons why. Seeing him with his son, with his other employees, playing ball and having him talk to her had touched her. She liked Reid as she had the day he rescued her from the flood.

With a half laugh of surprise, she realized she was... attracted to him, but the attraction would bring her nothing but grief. With a defeated sigh, she lay back on the lounge and tried to make her mind a blank.

SHE DRESSED with extra care the next day in a tailored beige linen suit and white blouse with a bow-tied neck. Her shining hair was French-braided severely with the end pinned under. When she emerged from her bedroom, Roxie looked at the outfit and then at her own loosely belted cotton dress.

"You appearing before the Supreme Court today?"

A grim smile curved Kathryn's lips. "As a matter of fact, I might be."

Roxie's eyes flickered. "You don't think he'd fire you over such a minor thing, do you?"

"No, I guess not."

"He'd be making a mountain out of a molehill."

"I dare you to tell him that to his face," Kathryn said, cheered by her friend's loyalty. "But knowing you, you'd do it."

Roxie shrugged and headed into the kitchen to grab some toast for breakfast. More slowly Kathryn followed, her mind leaping ahead to when she would have to face Reid. She would treat him as coolly as he treated her, she decided. Total professionalism would be her goal.

As it turned out, all her mental preparations were unnecessary. A note, scrawled in black slashes that must have pained Reid's penmanship teachers, told her he had gone to Phoenix on emergency business to do with the new property he'd acquired. He would return Tuesday afternoon.

Not sure whether to be let down or relieved, Kathryn folded the note and tucked it into her desk. If she didn't know better, she would have thought *he* was avoiding *her*. Fat chance, she chided herself and looked up to see Roxie's sympathetic gaze on her.

"He's gone for a couple of days," Kathryn said, keeping her voice brisk. "That'll give us time to finish the data-entry training manual. Let's take the completed sections into Reid's conference room and use the table to collate them."

As they worked, Kathryn was deep in thought, while Roxie chattered on about how fascinating the manual sounded. She said she was going to get Lydia Martinez, the data processing supervisor, to show her how to use the company's big mainframe computer. Absently Kathryn agreed that it sounded like a good idea.

She didn't guess what havoc her tacit agreement would cause until a white-faced Lydia rushed into her office the next day.

"Do you have any idea what that girl has done?" she demanded, pointing to a startled Roxie. "She's erased three months of sales history!"

Kathryn dropped the letters she'd been opening. "What?"

Roxie leaped to her feet. "I couldn't have! I don't know enough about the big computer to do something like that."

Looking incensed, Lydia clapped her hands onto her narrow hips. She was a tiny Filipino woman with a temper that belied her diminutive stature. "Well, *somebody* did it, and you're the only novice who's been fooling with the computer."

"Well, *you* let me!" Roxie fired back.

"Wait, wait, wait." Kathryn waved her hands in the air as if to cool their blazing tempers. "Don't you have the information on a backup disk?"

"No." Lydia gave Roxie a dark look. "The disk it was supposed to be on must have been flawed. It's somehow been erased."

Looking ill, Roxie sank into her chair. "Oh, I'm so sorry. I don't know how it happened. I didn't do it on purpose."

Lydia's fury seemed to cool as quickly as it had ignited. "I know. I was foolish to let you use the computer, but you seemed so eager and when you said you had Kathryn's permission to learn, I—"

"*My* permission? When did I...?" Kathryn's voice trailed off as she remembered the half-heard conversation she had shared with Roxie. Her heart felt as though it had plunged into her stomach, and she wondered dismally if she would have time to call her parents and tell them goodbye before Reid strangled her. "Oh...yes," she said faintly, "I remember." She took a deep breath. "Well, what can we do to fix this?"

"We'll have to go through all the old invoices and scratch sheets and key the information again. It'll take weeks." Lydia's grimace underlined the amount of work that faced her department.

"I'll help," Roxie said. "It's the least I can do."

"I will, too," Kathryn added, walking over to put an arm around Lydia's slumped shoulders.

Lydia looked up, a hint of amusement on her face. "Neither of you know how to key."

"Isn't that the truth?" Roxie moaned, sinking back into her chair.

"Well, there must be something we can do," Kathryn insisted.

Lydia pulled away and headed for the door. "You can help locate invoices." She leveled a look at Kathryn's pale face. "You can also talk Reid Darwin into authorizing overtime."

Kathryn could almost hear the nails being driven into the coffin containing her secretarial career. "Sure, Lydia," she said faintly, returning to her chair.

Roxie propped her elbows on her desk and rested her face in her hands. "Oh, Kath, I'm so sorry. I should have listened to you. I'm not right for this job."

Trying to rally from her own dark thoughts, Kathryn murmured, "No, it's not your fault. You just made a mistake."

Roxie's hands dropped palms up onto the desktop. She stared at them. "It seemed so simple. How could I possibly have erased three months of information?"

Her mind in a whirl, Kathryn tried to think. "Well, at least it was only three months' worth, and—what are you doing?"

Roxie had risen to her feet and pulled her purse from the desk drawer. "I'm quitting. I'll talk to personnel about my final paycheck." She paused, shaking her head, so that her long brown hair swished over her shoulders. "My first and final paycheck. I'll help out with the invoices on my own time."

Alarmed, Kathryn sprang up. "Rox, you can't do that. There's no need. You're doing fine in everything else...."

"Maybe so, but this is going to get you in deep trouble with Iron Eyes and we both know it. I don't mean to run out on you, but it's probably best if I'm not around to cause you more problems."

One shock on top of another had Kathryn reeling. She knew she couldn't let Roxie quit like this. "You won't!"

Color was beginning to come back into Roxie's face. She seemed grimly determined. "Listen...you call up a temporary employment agency and tell them you don't want any more of their second-string typists. You need someone with the best skills. I'll write your boss a note telling him exactly what happened so he'll know to blame me."

"You don't have to do this," Kathryn insisted, standing by her desk.

"Yes, I do. I promised I'd quit if I caused you any problems." She sighed. "And this is a doozie!"

Before Kathryn could argue further, the phone started ringing. Her eyes full of tears, she dealt distractedly with the caller while Roxie dashed off a note to Reid and rushed in to leave it on his desk.

Roxie returned, grabbed her purse and mouthed, "I'll take the bus home." With a shaky smile, she hurried out.

Kathryn didn't have to wait long for Reid's reaction. He returned from Phoenix while she was at lunch. She was just putting her purse away and getting out her afternoon's work when he came striding into her office. With one hand he swept the door shut and with the other waved Roxie's note in front of Kathryn.

"Is this true?" he demanded, puzzlement and anger warring on his face.

Kathryn nodded, her gaze skimming his features, which were harsher than ever. "Yes, I'm afraid so. It was an accident, though. She couldn't possibly have known the backup disk was blank, too."

Reid drew back. Disbelief won the battle as the overriding emotion on his face. "Yes, she says here it was an accident. So why on earth did you fire her?"

# CHAPTER FIVE

KATHRYN'S MOUTH dropped open and her voice came out in a Katydid-like squeak. "Fire her? Is that what the note says?"

She made a grab for the paper as it swung past her face, but Reid snapped it around and read the last part of it to her.

"'I'm sorry about this, Reid, and I'll try to rectify the situation. I'm leaving as I said I would.'" He glared at Kathryn. "We don't fire employees for a first mistake, even one this severe."

"I did *not* fire her," Kathryn said tightly, reining in her temper. "Before she took this job she insisted she'd quit if she did anything to cause problems."

Honestly! she thought, seething. She had been so sure he would be angry about Roxie's mistake. Instead he was mad for an entirely different reason. Kathryn felt condemned if she did and condemned if she didn't!

She looked down at her hands, fully aware of her own role in the disaster. "I'm partly responsible, though," she said, explaining her inattention when Roxie asked about using the big computer. If Reid had needed anything to confirm his bad opinion of her he had it now.

Kathryn watched his face as she talked and saw his disbelief and confusion harden into annoyance. Reid speared his fingers through his hair. She noticed that the lines bracketing his mouth were deeper than ever and that exhaustion shadowed his eyes. Immediately she was piqued with herself for noticing and caring. When she finished speaking there was silence for a moment, as if he was gathering his thoughts, then he said, "All right. What's going to be done to take care of this mess?"

Kathryn told him about Lydia's plan and he nodded, listening.

When she had finished, he folded Roxie's note with quick, sharp creases and nodded. "Good. See that it's solved as soon as possible." He turned on his heel, ready to leave, but Kathryn stopped him.

"Reid, there's something else."

He turned back, one hand on the door, the other on his hip in a stance that exuded impatience. "What is it?"

She pushed her palms together briefly, then straightened her shoulders. "Lydia—well, *I* would need you to authorize overtime to clear this up."

His eyes widened as if he couldn't believe what he was hearing, then narrowed as if he was mentally calculating how much this folly was going to cost his company.

Though she wished she could, Kathryn didn't back down. Her eyes met his without flinching. "Of course, Roxie and I will work without pay since we're responsible."

Kathryn detected a flicker of warmth in him. "Sounds like you've covered all the bases." The softening she saw in his expression disappeared. "But if you'd covered everything in the first place, this wouldn't have happened."

Even knowing that his statement was justified didn't take the sting from his words. She had already apologized. Kathryn's chin poked out.

He watched her defensive gesture, said, "The overtime is authorized," and stalked out.

Kathryn followed him and shut her office door so she could have some peace and quiet. *He* hadn't spoken a word of apology for wrongly accusing her of firing Roxie. Oh, no. She stomped across to her desk and began rearranging her stack of work.

Maybe she should be grateful that at least he hadn't mentioned the picnic. That would probably have set him off even more. Not that he had any right to be upset, she added, with a self-righteous sniff.

Her nervous fingers adjusted the angle of the miniblinds at her window. Perhaps she should just quit, too, she thought. Then he could find someone who suited him. But Jill was depending on her, and Kathryn knew she handled most parts of the job without a problem. Unfortunately the blunders, rare though they were, overshadowed her competence. But she had already decided never again to be driven from a job she liked.

The knowledge that her thirty-day review would be coming up in the next few days niggled at the back of her mind. This disaster would surely have an impact on that.

Restlessly she picked up a folder of forms she needed to mail to the health insurance company. Roxie would have handled this chore if she had stayed. Now she would have to do both jobs again until she found someone. Kathryn flipped the file open to see how many copies needed to be returned to the personnel department.

The name Sean Darwin caught her eye, and she pulled out the form. After throwing a guilty look over her shoulder, she scanned the page. It was a standard form, giving the date and time of Sean's recent visit to a group of ear specialists, with the diagnosis sheet attached.

Frowning in concentration, she worked to decipher the doctors' handwriting. In the opinion of the doctors and the audiologist, Sean was too profoundly deaf to benefit from the use of hearing aids. It was recommended that he begin intensive speech therapy as soon as possible. Because Sean was of above-average intelligence, the doctors felt he could at least learn to speak and achieve a more normal life.

When Kathryn was finished, she held the sheets to her, bending her head down so that her thick hair hid her face. Tears sprang to her eyes and squeezed out from beneath her tightly shut lids.

Sean would never have a completely normal life. Kathryn thought of Maxie, her friend from her circus days. Although his life had been full and happy, he had sometimes struggled against his own frustrations and other people's prejudices. Sean seemed well adjusted, but it hurt her to think of him experiencing pain.

And although she didn't like being the target of Reid's irritation, maybe she could understand some of his feelings. He was a widower struggling to raise a handicapped child. Disasters at work only added to the stress in his life—and she had helped create a disaster. She reached for a tissue and dabbed at her eyes.

A perfunctory knock sounded on her office door and it swung open. "Kathryn, could you bring your pad and..." Reid paused when she whipped around, presenting her back to him and furiously wiping her eyes.

"I'll be right there," she said, her voice wavering with a shakiness she despised.

"Kathryn? What's wrong?" He came into her office and shut the door behind him. When she didn't answer, he crossed the room and touched her shoulder tenderly.

Kathryn drew away, too aware of how foolish she must look, standing there crying. "Nothing," she said with a defensive tightness in her voice. "I said I'd be right there—if you'll give me a minute to get my things."

Reid ignored her attempts to pull away from him. One of his big hands clasped her shoulder and turned her toward him. His other hand reached out to lift her chin with the tips of two fingers. Her teary eyes were forced to meet his troubled ones.

"I don't have to ask if it was something I said." His voice was a deep, concerned rumble. "It was everything I said, wasn't it?"

Kathryn blinked. Everything he'd said? Oh, he thought she was crying because of the harsh way he had spoken to her about Roxie. She voiced her thoughts. "No, Reid, I'm not crying because of that."

What looked like a spasm of regret clenched his face, emphasizing the harsh lines. The fingers that tilted her jaw slipped around so that they cupped her small pointed chin. He hesitated, and then, as if he couldn't help himself, he slid his thumb over her velvety cheek and across her bottom lip.

Her mouth parted in surprise, and pleasure speared through her. Pure delight leaped into her eyes, intensifying the gold cast over green. "Reid..." His name trembled out of her.

Reid's thumb made another pass over her lips. "I apologize, Kathryn."

It would be so easy, she thought, to believe the warmth in his eyes. But she wasn't sure she dared.

"I know I'm the devil to work for sometimes," he went on, his voice rumbling in a faintly regretful tone. His thumb continued its exploration of her creamy skin, running along her jawline then skimming up by her ear and over her cheekbone, coming to rest just below her eye.

Kathryn's lashes fluttered down as awareness of him filled her senses. The warmth of his thumb rested on her skin. A deep breath shuddered into her lungs, bringing with it the tangy scent of his cologne. She was reminded of the day of the flood when he had carried her across the bridge and she had buried her nose in his neck. Her eyes drifted open, anticipating what would happen next.

To her bemusement, his thumb stilled and slowly drew away. His hand followed and the momentary warmth and concern she had seen in his expression was blown away as if before a frosty wind. He was looking down at her desk.

Floundering to keep pace with the sudden change in atmosphere, she turned her head to follow the direction of his gaze.

Reid had caught sight of the papers she'd been holding. He must have noticed his son's name, too, because he reached out and snatched them up.

"What's this?"

"Insurance forms I have to mail in."

"About Sean?" His voice was deadly calm, but it sent a frisson of alarm up Kathryn's spine.

"Yes."

Reid studied her face, his eyes tracking the faint smudges tears had made under her eyes. "Don't cry for him. Tears won't change a thing."

Puzzled, Kathryn stared at him, trying to decipher his harsh tone, but he turned and began striding out. "Now," he said, "I've got letters to get out."

The afternoon provided a subtle shift in their relationship. Reid seemed to have lost a little of his critical attitude, but she often found him peering into her office, watching her. It didn't ease her mind any that his look was faintly puzzled.

The next day Kathryn hired another junior secretary sent out by a temporary employment agency. Although young, Brianna Wiggins had good skills. She had masses of auburn hair, a bright smile and a quick swinging walk that soon had the sales reps following her down the halls.

After her experience with Roxie, Kathryn had decided the office was too small for both of them. She nervously weighed the advantages of having the office to herself against the memory of what her inattention to Roxie's shenanigans had caused. Brianna seemed more suited to office work than Roxie was, though, and was very conscientious. Kathryn moved her to a small empty office down the hall, and the two women settled into a routine that suited them both, plowing through the piled-up work.

In the afternoons and on weekends Kathryn and Roxie helped the data processing department sort out the mess Roxie had made. It was cleared up within two weeks, and Roxie returned to her job hunting.

During one especially busy morning, Reid called Kathryn into his office. Since it was the third time he had done so that day, Kathryn clicked her tongue impatiently, gave a fleeting look to the stack of work on her desk, grabbed her stenographer's pad and some pencils and hurried to him.

He waved her to a chair and continued reading through some papers on his desk.

She tried not to fidget while she waited for him, but found herself repeatedly smoothing the skirt of her blue seersucker suit across her knees.

Finally Reid lifted his head, his clear eyes surveying her for a moment. "Would you be my date this Friday night?"

Kathryn couldn't have been more surprised if he'd vaulted over his desk and kissed her. She barely kept her jaw from sagging. "Date?"

Reid stood and walked over to shut his office door, moving without hurry as if he was giving her time to consider. He returned to his desk and sat down, crossing his shirtsleeved arms across his chest. "Yes," he said, without elaborating.

"This Friday?"

His blunt features were unreadable. "I imagine you have other plans. If you could change them, I would make it worth your while."

"Well, I don't know..." she began, aware of the quick upthrust of pleasure that had darted through her when she heard his request. She could hardly believe they were having this conversation and, of course, she couldn't seriously consider going out with her boss. The office grapevine would be absolutely sizzling.... It was a terrible idea.... She couldn't do it.

"I suppose I could change my plans," Kathryn said, breaking into an eager smile.

He gave her one of his characteristic quick nods, but his eyes lingered on her lips.

Nervous excitement beat within her. "But do you think this is a good idea, Reid—what with office gossip and—"

"Gossip?" Now it was his turn to look surprised. He tilted his head, causing a lock of rich brown hair to fall across his forehead.

Good grief, did she have to spell it out for him? Sure he was a widower and she was single, but they were still boss and secretary.

"Because you own this company," she began, dropping her pad and pencil in her lap and spreading her hands to encompass the room. "You're my boss."

Reid looked at her as if she'd suddenly begun speaking Swahili. "I don't see that it's anyone else's business. There will be others there."

Others? She couldn't stop the consternation that flashed across her face when she realized what he was talking about. How could she have forgotten? She had made the arrangements herself. It was a business dinner! Embarrassed, but determined to hide it, she crossed her legs demurely and smoothed her cotton skirt once again. "Yes, of course. As I recall, there will be twelve couples attending, right?"

Reid looked as if he wanted to say something about her silly misconception, but the proud upthrust of her peaked chin signaled him to let it pass.

"Yes," he finally said. "Some longtime vendors and some new ones with products they want to sell me. My mother was going to be the hostess, but she can't make it, after all. I'll pick you up at your place at six-thirty. You can leave the office early that day if you need the time to get ready." Dismissively he picked up the stack of papers he had been studying.

Kathryn arched her brows, irritated by his unspoken dismissal. "That won't be necessary," she said, standing up. "I'll just borrow Roxie's red tights. It shouldn't take me long to get ready."

His eyes snapped to hers. "What's that supposed to mean?"

"It means I'll be glad to come and help out in any way I can. If you want me as hostess I'll be the best darned hostess you ever saw."

Reid stared at her for a moment, then his firm mouth twitched up in the slightest of smiles. "But I could be a little more appreciative? Why did I expect you to express your gratitude for the invitation, curtsy politely and hurry out?" he asked, shaking his head.

It took a few seconds for Kathryn to find her voice. "I don't know. I've certainly never done anything like that in my life. I would break my own hand before I would tug my forelock."

"You wouldn't have to go quite that far!" Reid said and gave a short laugh. He planted his hands on top of the desk, stood suddenly and swept her a courtly bow that had her staring at him openmouthed. "Miss Evans, would you do me the honor of accompanying me Friday night? I would be most grateful."

"I would be delighted." She intended to sweep regally from the room, but he stopped her.

"Kathryn?"

Turning back, she saw that he was drumming his fingers on the desktop. His eyes were narrowed in thought. "About that thirty-day review. Let's call it done. I'll tell personnel to upgrade your salary."

"Upgrade? Why, thank—thank you." She would have said more, but his phone rang. With a dismissive nod he picked it up, and she walked out of his office, wondering when she would ever understand him.

He had waived the thirty-day review! That had seemed so important to him a few weeks ago, but now he had dismissed it. She shook her head. Although she was delighted that her work seemed to please him at last, she was stunned by his change in attitude—not to mention his invitation to the dinner.

She probably shouldn't have agreed to go, even if he did need a hostess. Then she recalled what he had been like at the company picnic, friendly and approachable. Although she knew he probably wouldn't be like that again, she couldn't stifle the warm glow she felt at the thought of being alone with him, away from work. She all but skipped into her office.

ON FRIDAY EVENING Kathryn swung the door open at Reid's knock. He stood with one hand on the doorjamb, the other in his pocket and stared at her. His black dinner jacket, she noticed, was perfectly cut, emphasizing the breadth of his shoulders and the rich darkness of his hair.

His gaze rested for a long time on her, taking in the curly red mass of hair she'd pulled back on one side and secured with a silk passion flower, and roaming to the other side, where her hair fell across her cheek, contrasting with the milky fairness of her skin.

"No red tights?" He smiled faintly, casting a meaningful glance to her legs.

She couldn't believe he was actually teasing her. "Roxie wouldn't share," she said, giving him a playful look from beneath lowered lashes. Completely unnerved by his scrutiny, she fidgeted with the gossamer skirt of her seafoam-green gown and shifted back a step or two.

The dress was her favorite. It had spaghetti straps and a sweetheart neckline that bared her creamy shoulders. The snug-fitting bodice and wide skirt emphasized her narrow waist.

She gestured toward the living room. "Would you like to come in?"

Her question seemed to take a moment to sink in. She watched his gaze drift over her once again before lifting to her face. The tips of her ears went cold and hot by turns, and she felt light-headed with a joyousness that brightened her eyes and broadened her smile. Oh, she thought, this was going to be a great evening, with her grinning like a jack-o'-lantern whenever he looked in her direction!

Reid finally broke the eye contact and glanced inside. "How's the circus act?"

"I beg your pardon?"

"Your drop-dead dog."

"Oh, Bosco. He's fine. He and Hellion actually like each other."

"Great," Reid said, his smile transforming the firm line of his mouth. "Maybe you can train them to do tricks together."

She smiled at the inane chatter they were sharing. "Maybe I will."

Reid lifted his hand in an uncharacteristically open gesture and his voice warmed a tone. "You know, my son loves animals. He would love to meet these two."

"Would he? Why don't you bring him over someday?" she suggested eagerly. "Bosco knows tons of tricks and sometimes he even gets them right!"

They laughed together for a moment and then grew silent, looking at each other. Kathryn thought he was very appealing with his usually reserved expression softened by a smile.

Finally, he broke the eye contact and said, "I think we'd better be on our way. We'll need to check arrangements."

"Of course." Kathryn picked up her purse and a light wrap from the table in the hall.

Reid took the shawl from her. He looked down in some surprise when it seemed to drape itself intimately around his hand. Kathryn's lips curved at his startled look.

The white fabric was a silk knit cunningly designed by a craftswoman she had met when the circus played in North Carolina.

Reid's blunt features had gone completely blank, but his gray eyes held a luminous beam. His thumb jerked over the slick-sensuous stuff—as if propelled by desire and dragged by reluctance. He then crushed the shawl gently in his fist, and slowly, his eyes lifted to hers.

Kathryn saw yearning in his gaze. The heat that had been localized in the tips of her ears washed down her body, and she released a startled breath.

Faint as it was, the sound seemed to bring Reid back to reality. He looked down at the shawl as if he couldn't imagine what he was supposed to do with it. She whipped around so he could place the garment across her shoulders, and he dropped it into place like a hot coal.

Kathryn gulped in air. "Thank you. Shall we go?"

He grunted his acknowledgment and led her out to his Chrysler New Yorker. When he had helped her into the leather seat and they had started off, he asked, "Aren't your roommates at home?"

Kathryn settled more comfortably into the luxurious seat. "Roxie went to a movie with friends. Wilma is at the Stewart Art Gallery."

"Oh, looking at an exhibit?"

"No-o-o." Kathryn dragged out the word.

"Is she an artist?"

"Not exactly." Kathryn inspected the residences on Raymond Road as if she had never seen them before. "She's . . . demonstrating." Deliberately she muffled the last word, but his hearing was sharper than she had thought.

"Demonstrating?"

Kathryn cleared her throat. "Maybe protesting would be a more accurate word. There's an art show there tonight, and she and her cronies are upset because wealthy art patrons don't give enough money to help the homeless."

Kathryn watched the corner of Reid's mouth. When it twitched upward, she relaxed. He was obviously remembering his encounter with the feisty older lady. He asked if Roxie had found a new job and Kathryn said she was still looking.

To her pleased surprise, Reid asked her how she'd joined the circus and Kathryn told him that Roxie's stories about her grandmother's life in the circus had been so intriguing they both decided to join when they were old enough.

Reid listened intently, making comments and asking questions. Kathryn felt flattered. She could almost think there had never been a harsh word between them.

Before she knew it, they were at the El Conquistador Inn, Tucson's newest hotel. The entrance was massive, with big white columns supporting the porch roof. The drive was paved in red concrete squares that resembled Spanish tiles.

Kathryn had never been to the inn before and she looked around with eager anticipation. A white-jacketed valet opened the door of Reid's New Yorker and assisted Kathryn to the sidewalk, then darted around to the driver's side and took the wheel.

Inside they were led to a private room where they were soon joined for cocktails by Reid's guests. Kathryn was pleasantly surprised to learn she knew several of the guests due to their visits to the office. She began to relax.

Reid was in the middle of a group of vendors, talking sales strategy, and Kathryn was chatting with several of the women when she was approached by a dark-haired man with an easy smile and intense blue eyes.

"Do I dare hope the most beautiful woman at the party is here alone?" he asked in a pleasantly husky voice.

Kathryn laughed and shook her head, amazed at the man's boldness and blatant flattery. "I'm Reid Darwin's secretary," she said, holding out her hand. "Kathryn Evans."

Immediately the man's eyes lit with interest as he took her hand and shook it. "Please tell me there's no Mr. Evans."

Kathryn's eyes sparkled with humor. Really! She had heard her share of lines, but this was straight out of the movies. "My father is Mr. Evans," she replied easily. "He and my mother live in Springerville."

The man nodded, his gaze traveling over her face, taking in the sweep of her dress. "I remember talking to you on the phone when your boss canceled an appointment with me. My name's Jared Sykes." He paused, watching her. "So you have the great man's ear, hmm?"

The great man? What a strange way to put it. She remembered speaking to Sykes her first day in Jill's job. He had sounded very irritated, but she'd had little time to soothe him. "Well, as I said, I work for him."

"What happened to his other secretary?"

"She's taken a temporary leave of absence for health reasons. She'll return in a few months."

Jared's smile was warmly approving. "And you've stepped into the breach. How commendable. Say, would you care to be my partner at dinner? I'd like to tell you all about a new product I'm developing that might interest your boss. Maybe you can put in a good word for me."

So that was the reason for the flattery. It had never occurred to her that she would ever be in the position of being courted because of her proximity to Reid. "I'm here with my boss. I imagine I'll sit with him."

Sykes grinned. "Save me a dance after dinner, then." He winked and drifted away just as a waiter entered to announce that their tables were ready.

Kathryn felt her elbow being caught from behind, and a warm tingling sensation that was becoming achingly familiar told her it was Reid.

"Who is that guy?" he rasped in her ear.

She glanced up in surprise. The pleasant expression he had shown her earlier had been replaced with narrow-eyed interest. "You mean you don't know him?

He says his name is Jared Sykes. Didn't you invite him?''

"Oh, so that's Jared Sykes." Reid favored her with a downward glance. "Yes, I've canceled appointments with him three times in the past two weeks so I decided the least I could do was invite him tonight. With a lot of other people around I can cut his spiel short."

"His spiel? What does he want?"

He leaned close as she seated herself so that no one else could hear. His breath was a warm puff against her ear. "At the moment I'd say he wants you."

Kathryn's eyes flew to his face, but he was already turning away. Before she could regain his attention, she found herself having to make small talk with the wife of a paper products distributor on her left while all of her thoughts were centered on the man to her right.

After the prime rib dinner, Jared Sykes made good on his promise and approached her to dance. Maybe he did come on strong, Kathryn reasoned, but he was an excellent dancer, and she loved to dance. Because of the years she had spent in tumbling and juggling in a group, she could sense a partner's lead and follow it easily. And Sykes was very easy to follow.

As she had anticipated, he talked enthusiastically while they danced. She found herself liking him because he was friendly and funny, and she really didn't mind when he began talking business again, but she was caught off guard when he asked for her help.

"Can you make an appointment that your boss will keep?" Jared asked, getting right to the point.

Kathryn glanced at him uneasily and then over at Reid who was watching them. "You'd have to talk to

Reid about this yourself," she began, casting about mentally for a diplomatic way to tell him how little influence she really had with her boss. The poor man looked so disappointed that she found herself adding, "He's been very busy, but he seems to be talking business tonight."

"I don't want to talk with all these people here." Jared glanced around the room. "Maybe I'll call him Monday."

To Kathryn's immense relief he then dropped the subject and began telling her a witty story about his college chemistry classes.

Kathryn danced with him several times, as well as with some of the other men. Reid never asked her—he seemed too busy—but she felt him watching her, especially when she was with Jared.

Once when she danced past him in Jared's arms, she raised her eyebrows in puzzled question. Reid tilted his head as if questioning her, too.

She found out what had been on his mind once the last guest left and they were settled in Reid's car for the drive home.

Keeping his eyes on the road he said, "I'd be careful of that situation if I were you."

The evening had been fun. Kathryn was feeling pleasantly tired and mellow from the number of dances she had danced and the two glasses of wine she had drunk. She rested her head on the top of the seat and turned her face to him, smiling. "What situation?"

"Sykes."

She straightened. "As far as I'm concerned, there's no situation with Jared Sykes."

Reid's eyes seemed to flash like silver lances as he looked over at her. "He likes you."

"Is that a crime?"

"It's always a mistake to become involved with anyone we do business with."

"Involved! I just met the man."

"You'll be seeing him again."

He sounded so dead sure, Kathryn's lips thinned in irritation. "And you don't want me to?"

He shrugged one massive shoulder. "It's never a good idea to mix business with pleasure."

Rebelliously Kathryn sat back and crossed her arms. She had enjoyed herself this evening, and Reid was ruining it with this ridiculous talk. "Reid, he was a guest at your party. Would you have preferred that I glare at the man all evening?" *Like you did,* she added silently.

"No," he snapped, swinging the car a little too fast around a corner. "Just don't let him take advantage of your association with me."

Kathryn stared at him. As if she ever would! Hurt, she turned her head and stonily faced the windshield.

When they got to her house, Kathryn was all ready to say a quick good-night, jump out of the car and rush inside, but a steady look from Reid told her she had better stay where she was until he opened her door for her. Only a porch light was burning, and as they walked toward her front door, Kathryn heard the phone ring. Neither roommate appeared to be home yet, so she said, "I'd better get that," and hurriedly unlocked the door.

Bosco and Hellion greeted her as she hurried in, then turned to sniff around Reid's shoes. They decided to be friendly when he knelt down and scratched them behind their ears. "No thunderstorms to make me look like an enemy tonight, hmm, you two?"

Kathryn could still hear his rumbling voice as she picked up the receiver. She talked for only a moment before she dropped the phone back on its cradle and dashed toward the front door.

"I've got to run, Reid. Thank you for asking me to go with you tonight," she said, forgetting they had just had an argument. "I enjoyed it very much."

He was instantly alert, his gray eyes searching her distracted face. "Run? Run where?"

"Jail," she said, scrabbling in her purse for her car keys. "Wilma's been arrested!"

# CHAPTER SIX

"ARRESTED?" Reid thundered the word at her.

Kathryn waited impatiently by the front door for him to unglue his big feet from her entryway and leave so she could lock the house. "That's right. Apparently she and her cronies didn't have a permit for their demonstration. I should have known," she added on a sigh.

"And now she's in jail, waiting for you to bail her out?"

"That's right." Kathryn's hand made a little flick toward the front door. "Reid, I don't mean to be rude, but I've got to go."

His gaze narrowed on her for a second. "I'll drive you."

"No!" The last thing she needed was for him to get involved in this mess.

"Don't argue. Let's go." This time it was Reid who waited impatiently by the front door.

At least he's outside, she thought. Whipping the door shut, she locked it and hurried across the porch. "This isn't necessary. I can handle it."

"It'll be easier if you have help," he said calmly, taking her arm and stuffing her gently back into the New Yorker. "Do you have bail money?"

She groaned. "Oh, no, I didn't think . . ."

"I'll take care of it," he said, rounding to his own side and climbing in. "Wilma can pay me back. Now, where is she being held?"

Kathryn told him and they started off. A few minutes later he asked, "Does she do this kind of thing often?"

"Constantly," Kathryn sighed. "I just wish she hadn't gotten arrested this time."

"Just how many times has this happened?"

Kathryn chewed her bottom lip, wrecking her carefully applied lipstick. "Twice," she finally admitted. "I was with her once."

His head sprang around toward her. "You were?"

"Charges were dropped," she hurried to add. "The owners of the place knew I wasn't really one of the demonstrators."

Reid nodded slowly, listening hard, as if any second now the conversation would start making sense. "And how did they know that?"

"I was the only one there under sixty."

The traffic light before them flashed to red. Reid stopped, tucked his big right shoulder into the rich leather and leaned toward her. "What was she protesting that time?"

"Poor care of the elderly at a convalescent home that had a reputation for carelessness."

"Why were you there?"

Kathryn threw her hands wide. "Well, somebody had to watch out for her."

"And you were elected? Who were the voters?"

"I volunteered. Roxie was in bed with a sprained ankle, so I went, but Wilma said she didn't want us interfering with her causes anymore."

"Damned sensible. Has she always been like this?"

"No, not when she had an exciting job and an audience every day," Kathryn answered candidly. She went on to explain Wilma's fears of not being needed.

"Do your parents know what's been going on down here since they left?"

"I'm an adult, Reid. I've been on my own for seven years. My parents don't have to watch out for me."

His hands gripped the wheel. "Somebody should. People take advantage of you."

"Who takes advantage of me?"

He shrugged. "People at work. Your roommates. They probably don't intend to, but you make it easy for them."

Kathryn didn't want to get into an argument with him—especially since he was helping her bail Wilma out—so she kept quiet until they reached the police station.

Inside, Wilma and her friends were in a holding cell. Their protest signs had been taken away from them and were leaning against a beat-up file cabinet.

"Which one's yours?" asked a beefy sergeant as his weary eyes surveyed the two in evening clothes.

"The one in the purple jogging suit who's trying to pick the lock," Reid answered, surveying the motley group.

The officer turned and glared at Wilma.

She spotted them at that moment, withdrew her hand and her hairpin from the lock and called out, "Kathryn, dear, how nice to see you!"

Kathryn walked up to the cell and clapped her hands onto her hips. Tapping the toe of one high-heeled sandal, she said, "I should let you stay here. Roxie's going to have plenty to say to you, you know. Why didn't you get a permit if you were going to do this?"

"Because they wouldn't have given us one," Wilma answered guilelessly. "And this way has more impact."

"Yes," Reid said, coming up behind Kathryn. "On your pocketbook."

"Oh, hello, Mr. Darwin," Wilma said, cheerfully. "How nice to see you. Did you bring dear Kathryn down?"

"Dear" Kathryn rolled her eyes. Wilma sounded as if she and Reid had dropped by for tea and a game of croquet. She turned away to talk to the clerk about bail, but could still hear the conversation.

"Yes, I did, Mrs. Tarleton, and I think you'd better be grateful she was willing to come."

"Come on, everyone," Wilma went on, ignoring the unsubtle reprimand. "It looks like we've been sprung."

"We?" Kathryn squeaked. She could just imagine Reid spending thousands of dollars to bail this bunch out and never getting the money back. "Oh, no—your friends have to wait for their families."

Wilma protested, and Reid looked as if he was trying to hide a smile, but Kathryn was adamant. He should be grateful, she thought, because she had just saved him a lot of money. Instead, he was probably thinking that at least she was only being taken advantage of by one person in this situation and not half a dozen.

Bail was arranged, Reid wrote out a staggering check, and Wilma was released. She bounced out of the holding cell as if she had just gone through a great adventure. The families of her friends were arriving so she was willing to leave. Gratefully Kathryn hustled her outside and into Reid's car. Still high on adrena-line Wilma chattered all the way home.

Roxie's car was in the drive when they pulled up to the house, and she came out onto the porch.

"Grandma, what's going on?" she asked, her eyes going from person to person.

Wilma bounded to the front door. "Come on in, honey. I'll tell you all about it."

By this time it was one o'clock in the morning, and Kathryn was unutterably weary. Her shoulders drooped as she turned to say good-night. "Thank you for all you've done, Reid. I'll make sure Wilma pays you back right away."

His heavy brows rose and his eyes glinted. "Look on the bright side. Maybe they'll lock her up for a while so you can have a break from her. One way or another, your roommates cause you problems."

"But I love them," Kathryn said, tightly. "They're my best friends."

"Friends can take advantage of you. So can co-workers."

"And total strangers," Kathryn added, knowing where this was going.

"Yes, strangers like Sykes."

Kathryn's small pointed chin drew up. "I am your secretary, Reid. I won't let Jared in to see you if it's not what you want."

Reid swept back the sides of his jacket and dug his hands into his pockets. He rocked back on his heels as he regarded her in the porch light. "I'm not worried about that. I can take care of myself. The question is, can you? You seem to always want to make every-thing all right for people. And some things just can't be fixed. Life just isn't that simple."

Green eyes wide, Kathryn stared at him, marveling at the bitterness she heard underlying his tone.

Reid stared across the street where a light shone in a neighbor's window. The woman there suffered from insomnia, and Kathryn thought she probably spent time spying on the neighbors, too—at least she kept a pair of binoculars on a table by the window. The elderly lady was doubtless consumed with curiosity about what was going on. Kathryn sighed inwardly. *She* wasn't even sure what was going on.

"What do you mean, I try to make things all right for everybody? Despite what you think, I don't let people take advantage of me. I care about them...the employees at work, my roommates, my parents—" she studied his face, moving around boldly to see his eyes in the porch light. "Little boys with big blue eyes—" she took a deep breath, knowing he wouldn't like what she had to say. "And whether you like it or not, I care about *you*, too, Reid." She watched as a spasm contracted his mouth, drawing it and the corner of one eye down, as if he had received a blow.

His voice was gruff when he spoke. "You don't really even know me."

Though her hand shook slightly, she laid it on his sleeve. "Whose fault is that?"

She felt the muscles of his forearm jump as if he wanted to pull away. She didn't let go, though, hanging on stubbornly until he looked up and met her eyes.

Her lips quivered. "You remind me of someone easing himself into a tub of water. First the toe goes in, and it's jerked back. You try again and manage to get a foot in, then a leg, then the rest of you."

Reid answered her analogy with a rueful shake of his head. As if it was hard for him to admit, he said slowly, "At one time, I would have just taken the plunge. Maybe it's time I took the plunge again." He surprised her by capturing the hand that rested on his sleeve and pulling it up around his neck. His other hand sought the arm hanging limp at her side and drew that up, too. His hands went around her waist. They felt warm through her dress. Reid pulled her closer and bent his head.

Kathryn anticipated the kiss, and if thoughts of what a mistake it would be to get involved with her boss flew through her mind, she refused to pay attention. Eager for what was coming, she lifted her chin.

Their mouths met softly, slightly open and hesitant, as if neither person wanted to push this first kiss too far, too fast. Under her hands, Kathryn felt his shoulder muscles bunch and strain as if he was holding himself back. His mouth explored hers in a way that showed her he was willing to express desire but not to give too much warmth and tenderness.

Kathryn experienced excitement and arousal, a tingling shock to her senses when his lips nipped softly at hers. She wanted more, wanted him to deepen the kiss, but she felt that, although he had initiated the kiss, he wasn't willing to commit a certain part of himself to it. She felt the reserve in him. She brought her hand around and lay her palm along his cheek, then drew her lips away. The muscles in his jaw jerked when she spoke. "Whatever it was that hurt you so badly must have been terrible if you can't accept caring. I'm sorry, Reid. I'm very, very sorry."

Her words broke the spell as she had known they would, but they couldn't remain unspoken. Reid pulled back, letting his arms slip away as did hers.

"I survived," he said in a tone that threw her sympathy back at her. He turned and loped down the steps to the car.

"Did you?" she whispered as she watched him back out. He carried defensiveness like a shield, keeping others at bay.

She glanced across the street to where her neighbor's light was winking out and felt her hopes flicker in the same way. Turning, she went inside and shut the door.


ON MONDAY MORNING Kathryn hesitated outside Reid's office door. She would have to face him sometime. Somehow she knew he wouldn't mention their kiss. Maybe it wasn't worth mentioning, she thought with a pang of regret, because he had brushed aside what she had tried to offer—not just herself, but caring and understanding. Well, what else had she expected?

Pulling in a resolute breath, she marched into Reid's office with Wilma's check for the bail money. Before he spoke, she held up her hand. "In case you're wondering, no, I did not lend her the money." She couldn't resist a wicked grin. "You were right. When she wrote out this check I think she decided a life of crime would be too expensive."

Reid smiled, his blunt features shifting pleasantly. He seemed relaxed this morning and looked cool in his conservative gray suit and white shirt. "You really think this will stop her?"

"We should be so lucky," Kathryn sighed.

"Just so you don't try to serve her time for her."

Kathryn allowed her eyes to widen in innocence, and she answered fervently. "Oh, I won't, Reid. I'm going to try to bribe the judge into dropping the charges."

She heard him muttering, "Smart mouth" under his breath as she swept out to open the mail, congratulating herself on how easy that had been.

When she reached her office, Kathryn stumbled to a halt in the doorway. Jared Sykes was lounging in her visitor's chair, a sample case at his feet.

He jumped up and offered his winning smile. "Hello. Thought I'd just drop by instead of calling again. Do you think Mr. Darwin would have time to talk to me this morning?"

Dismayed, Kathryn gathered her wits. Dealing with uninvited visitors was a task she hadn't faced yet. "I'm not sure," she hedged. "Exactly what is this product you want to demonstrate for Reid?"

"It's called Citra-Clean—made from oranges."

"You're kidding!"

Jared's handsome face drew into an offended frown. "I would never joke about a formula I perfected myself."

Kathryn bit her lip. She hadn't meant to offend him. He was obviously sensitive about his product, and an interview with Reid seemed vital to him. "Wait right here. I'll see if Reid can work you in."

Kathryn hurried to Reid's office. When she explained about Sykes, he frowned. "I don't think—"

"Oh, Reid, can't you do something for him? At least listen to him? It might be worthwhile." Kathryn's pale skin flushed with earnestness. "It's very important to him."

Slowly Reid eased himself back against the chair, his faintly mocking gaze on her. "Another ugly duckling needing to be turned into a swan? Didn't I warn you?"

Chagrined, she nodded. Of course he had. They had nearly gotten into an argument over it. Oh, she had to agree, she did get carried away sometimes trying to ease the way for people. She turned away.

"Wait a minute, Kathryn."

She paused and turned around.

"I'll see him," Reid said, his voice gruff. "But next time use better judgment."

Kathryn winced, knowing she had made quite a blunder. "All right, Reid," she answered meekly and hurried to her office to send Jared in.

He offered his thanks, which she didn't really want at the moment. Reid's respect meant far more. Disgruntled with herself, she got down to work opening the mail. Perhaps as Reid said, she did need to use better judgment.

Deep in thought, she didn't hear Reid's door open until Jared appeared beside her desk. He looked crestfallen. "Thanks for getting me in to see him, Kathryn, even though it didn't do any good. Apparently his company already carries a similar product."

Despite the lecture she had just been giving herself, she couldn't help the sympathy that filled her. She stood and shook his outstretched hand. "Better luck next place you try."

Jared's face cleared measurably. "That's the way it goes sometimes. Hey, I really enjoyed dancing with you the other night. Can I call you sometime?" he asked, giving her a wink.

Behind him Reid loomed suddenly in the doorway. "Sorry to interrupt, but aren't you supposed to be in an accounting meeting?'' he asked, leveling his flinty gaze at Kathryn.

Hastily she looked at her watch and grabbed her pad and pencil. ''Oh, dear. Goodbye, Jared,'' she said, scurrying down the hall, half angry with Reid for his high-handed reminder and half glad he had saved her from having to hurt Jared's feelings.

''Goodbye, Mr. Sykes,'' she heard him say curtly.

Just before she ducked into the accounting department, she looked back to see Jared all but sprinting toward the back door, sample case in hand.

Reid was scowling at her. Kathryn lifted her chin and swept into the meeting.

Reid didn't mention her blunder again, and things smoothed out for a while, but by Tuesday of the next week, she was struggling to keep up. She loaded Brianna down with work, then raced to keep up with her own tasks.

She was beginning to make some progress when Reid stepped into her office. ''Kathryn, do you have my plane reservations for Los Angeles yet?''

Kathryn looked at him and couldn't help longing for the few pleasant moments they had shared Friday night. She suppressed a sigh and answered calmly. ''They should be here any minute. The travel agency is sending them over.''

''Did you use my frequent-flier discount?''

Kathryn took a firm grip on her temper. She had been making his plane reservations for the past seven months without one foul-up. ''Yes, and I got you the lowest possible fare.'' *Unless you want to walk,* she thought snidely.

''Great. Now how about my report. Finished yet?''

Kathryn's fingertips whitened around the pen she had been using. "No. I've been quite busy this morning. This trip has taken me as much by surprise as it has you," she added in a level voice she hoped concealed her pique.

There had been no letup since she had walked in that morning. The vice president of sales who had been slated to go to the distributors' conference had come down with some kind of summer flu, leaving Reid to take over the workshop the man had intended to teach.

"When do you think it will be ready?"

*About thirty minutes after you leave me alone to do it,* Kathryn thought with another surge of unusual peevishness. "Pretty soon," she said, looking up as he moved into the room. "Unfortunately all his notes are handwritten." She glanced down at the scribbled-in and scratched-over stack of papers, unable to imagine why it hadn't been typed much sooner.

"Our V.P. of Sales likes to keep things to himself until he's ready to present them." Reid was standing at the edge of her desk now, the crease of his blue slacks almost brushing the wood.

Kathryn kept her eyes on his. Her face felt stiff in her effort to keep from looking impatient. She lifted her hands and deliberately placed them in a relaxed position atop the desk.

Reid's gray eyes were studying her, their expression as changeable as smoke dispelled by the wind. He looked down at the vulnerable dip of her palm, then at the soft curve of her lips. "I'll be taking a lot of equipment with me and I'll need you to drive the Jeep to the airport to pick me up when I come in."

Kathryn didn't even try to mask her surprise. "Me?"

His mouth twitched at the rise in her voice. "If you don't mind. I'll be coming in at night. Ordinarily I'd ask the warehouse to send someone for me, but they're shorthanded on that shift. I guess I could take a cab, but I'll have a lot of stuff and . . ."

Kathryn smiled. "And you don't want to trust our equipment to the tender mercies of a cab driver."

His smile was slow in answering. "Yeah." He reached into his pocket and drew out his keys. Detaching one from the ring, he handed it to her. "Here. Pick the Jeep up anytime. I'll tell my mother to expect you to come take the car."

He didn't look away for a moment, and Kathryn wondered if his thoughts paralleled hers. It would be a very personal thing for her to drive his car, to sit where he sat, put her hands where he put his, adjust the seat and the mirrors to her much shorter height. It would certainly be more personal than working together in an office—but less so than a kiss. To her intense disappointment, he said, "Could you have that presentation on my desk as soon as it's done?" He whirled and strode out.

"No," she muttered, stung by the rebuff. "I planned to take it out for a stroll as soon as it's typed." Disgusted with her own hatefulness she grabbed the stack of notes and set to work.

He pulled her in all directions, while he didn't give an inch. She wanted to get to know him, while he tried to keep himself invulnerable. She was anxious to understand the reason for his ambivalent feelings—his moods swung back and forth like a metronome—but he never opened up. It hurt her, bothered her, but perversely made her more determined to discover his secrets. She sighed. Either she was just a little crazy, or she was a glutton for punishment.

Forcing her mind off that treadmill, she focused on the last few lines of the report. When her phone rang, she frowned, resenting the break in her concentration, and picked up the receiver.

"Hello, Kathryn, remember me?"

She cocked her head, trying to place the voice. "Jared?"

"The very same. It's been more than a week. I was wondering if you felt the need to get away from it all."

Guiltily, Kathryn's eyes darted in the direction of Reid's office. "Get away where?"

"Maybe to dinner Friday evening and that new play at the Catalina Theater? I understand it's pretty good."

Kathryn bit her lip. The review in the newspaper had said the play was great, and she had hoped to see it, but she had promised to pick Reid up at the airport. Besides, she really wasn't interested in dating Jared. "I don't know, Jared . . ."

A movement in her doorway pulled Kathryn's gaze in that direction. Reid stood there, impatiently tapping a roll of papers against his palm, his eyes reproachful.

Coloring fiercely, she stammered into the receiver. "Ah, I'm afraid I can't make it this time," she said, then immediately regretted her choice of words. She should have been more forceful in her refusal. Darn Reid for rattling her.

Jared voiced his regrets, promised to call again, just as she had feared, and hung up. She returned the phone to its cradle and glanced at her boss.

Reid's thick brows elevated toward the line of his tobacco-brown hair. With flying fingers she touched some keys on her computer and started it printing the report. She treated him to a level look.

His steady voice seemed to underscore the clatter of the printer. "If you do go out with Sykes, just remember, I've already turned down his product."

She grabbed her coffee mug and stood up. "All right, Reid," she snapped, coming out from behind her desk. "I won't make that mistake again." A few rapid steps would have carried her through the door, but he was blocking it. Short of bringing in one of the warehouse forklifts, she didn't think she could budge him, so she stood, running her index finger around the mug's porcelain rim.

"Good." He quit tapping the roll of papers on his palm and, crossing his arms across his chest, leaned against the doorjamb.

Kathryn wondered what he would say if she told him she had turned down a date so she could pick him up at the airport. "The presentation is almost finished printing. I'll have it right to you."

Raising his thick brown brows, he turned toward the hallway. "I know I can depend on you, even if your mind is on other things."

Kathryn made a face at his back.

FRIDAY EVENING Kathryn dressed in a kelly-green sundress and walked around the corner to a retirement home where she and her roommates often volunteered their time. The day of the flood she had entertained at a birthday party to honor one of its residents. She spent several hours doing magic tricks and leading a sing-along, then strolled home, humming Gershwin tunes.

As she walked in the door, Hellion tumbled forward to curl around her feet. Kathryn had to tread carefully to avoid stepping on her new pet. Bosco also trotted forward to greet her.

"Hello, guys," she said, patting Bosco before scooping up the kitten. Bosco whined and Hellion turned on a rumbling purr. "Next time I go over to Shady Lane Retirement Home, you two will have to come along as back-up chorus. You'd do great on 'Singing in the Rain.'"

Two pairs of eyes, brown and green, stared back at her wistfully.

"Mark it in your engagement calendars," she instructed, walking into the living room. The sound of voices from the kitchen had her pushing the door open and peering in curiously.

Wilma and three friends sat around the table, papers spread before them. They were so involved in a lively discussion that they didn't even look up.

"Something has to be done about this!" Wilma declared, poking her finger in the middle of what looked like a chart.

"Well, who's going to do it?" asked an elderly man whose hair was dyed an improbable shade of red.

"We are!"

Over the hubbub Kathryn detected footsteps behind her and turned to see Roxie approaching. She was wearing an old robe and slippers and carrying a thick paperback romance under her arm.

"What's going on?" Kathryn asked, stepping back into the living room and allowing the door to swing shut.

Roxie's brown eyes rolled heavenward. "You don't want to know."

Someone began thumping the table and talking in a low, furious tone.

"If there's going to be bloodshed," Kathryn said, "I'd better know now so we can contact the next of kin."

"Rather than continue her scattered efforts to save the world, Grandma has decided to concentrate on the plight of the elderly."

Kathryn looked wary. "How?"

A heartfelt groan came from Roxie's throat. "Who knows, but may The Force be with us! Since the Stewart Gallery dropped charges against her, there's no stopping her. How was your evening?" she asked, abandoning the subject of her grandmother's latest project and turning to curl up in an easy chair.

"Great. Everyone wondered where you were. Mr. Peebles wants you to come next week and sit on his lap."

Roxie burst out laughing. "I'll send Grandma. She's the one who's anxious to improve the plight of the elderly."

"Please don't. They might try to elope." Kathryn stood and brushed off her skirt. "Well, I'd better go."

Roxie sat up. "Where? You just got home. It's almost ten o'clock."

"To pick Reid up. I told you about it."

"Oh, well don't stay out too late."

"Yes, Mama."

Roxie chucked a throw pillow at her. "Well, somebody has to earn some money around here so we can keep bailing Grandma out of jail!"

Kathryn laughed and called goodbye as she hurried out to the Jeep. Although she had driven it home from Reid's house that afternoon, the big vehicle still intimidated her.

Kathryn settled into the driver's seat, imagining Reid's warm hands gripping the steering wheel where she now placed hers.

It took her twenty minutes to reach the nearly deserted airport. Reid was sprawled in a chair in the lounge, and his long legs were stretched out in front of him, resting on the briefcase stacked atop his carry-on luggage. His suit jacket had been tossed over the next chair, his collar was open and his tie pulled loose. The visual aid materials and equipment he had used in his presentation were beside him.

Kathryn stopped in front of him, touched by how tired he looked. Tenderness welled up within her when she saw his mussed hair, the faint dusting of whiskers on his face and the lines of exhaustion that bracketed his mouth. She leaned closer and smiled when she heard him snoring faintly.

She knew she should wake him. It was unfair to have such an advantage, watching him when his defenses were down and he wasn't in control, as he seemed compelled to be. She couldn't resist, though, because she needed a moment to let her feelings for him take the next step in the fitful tug-of-war that raged within her.

As though playing on a movie screen, her mind flashed back scenes—Reid's tenderness with Jill, rescuing Hellion, his pride in Sean, the quick irritation he showed her, as well as his occasional, surprising patience. Most of all she relived the kiss on her front porch. In his arms she had experienced a wild rush of feeling completely new to her. No one had ever affected her this way.

She was in love with him.

Love. Shaken, Kathryn sat down in the chair beside him, her gaze never leaving his sleeping face as the truth took root in her mind and began to grow. She couldn't pinpoint exactly when it had happened, but she felt a surge of frightening elation that it had.

Knowing she had to touch him, she laid a trembling hand on his arm. "Reid, wake up. It's Kathryn. I'm here to take you home."

His gray eyes snapped open as his feet tumbled off the briefcase and hit the floor, sliding him back in the seat. At the same time, his hands slapped down on the chair arms. He gazed around, disoriented.

Kathryn jerked her head back. "Reid, are you all right?"

He rubbed one massive hand across his face. Sighing, he leaned back again, regarding her through half-closed eyes. "Hell, no. Do I look all right?" He glanced around and she noticed that his eyes looked faintly glazed. For the first time Reid appeared to really see her. His gaze traveled up from her white sandals, over the full-skirted dress, to the halter top that bared her shoulders. "Did you turn down that date with Sykes because you had someone else lined up?"

"Twelve others, actually," she said, trying to sound casual. "Are you ready to go?"

He gave her a black look. "Sounds like fun. Let's find a skycap to help us with this stuff. Where's the Jeep?"

Her lips pulled down. She refused to lower herself to his level of grumpiness and snap that "The car is in the lot, of course.'' Instead, she turned and started through the doors to signal for help.

She could have fallen in love with anyone, she thought. But, oh, no, she had to go and fall for the toughest, most difficult man she'd ever met.

Once they had everything loaded and Reid had tipped the skycap, Kathryn held the keys out to him.

He shook his head and turned toward the passenger side. ''Please—you drive.''

Kathryn blinked in surprise. Most men she knew didn't like being driven around by a woman, especially if it was the man's car. But Reid wasn't like any other man she had ever met. She could never predict what he was going to do.

Confident now in her ability to drive the Jeep, she slid behind the wheel and started the motor. After she had paid the parking fee and pulled onto the road, she glanced over at Reid who was relaxing in the seat.

In spite of his comment about her date, he seemed different tonight—thoughtful. The guard he usually displayed when she was around seemed to have been dropped, or at least shifted a little. Or maybe she was looking at him through a rosy glow and was willing to make allowances.

She watched him angle his long legs into one position then another as he tried to get comfortable. He finally positioned his left ankle atop his right knee, so that his left knee angled toward her, then nestled his head into the dip between the edge of the seat back and the door.

He seemed to have forgotten her. Perhaps it was just as well. She didn't want him to know how aware she was of him so close to her elbow, how her nose was seeking out his indefinable male scent, or how her eyes kept peeking to see the glow from the streetlights on his bluntly carved features. Darn it, she didn't want him to know how much she had missed him this week. Tonight she'd even thought about him the whole time she was leading the sing-along at the retirement home.

Kathryn saw a movement out of the corner of her eye and turned her head to see Reid put his hand on the back of her seat. His big blunt fingers touched the ends of her hair where it spilled over the upholstery. The personal touch so surprised her, she blurted, "Are you all right?"

"You already asked me that."

"Well, are you?" she persisted. "You don't act like yourself."

"I'm just tired." He sighed. "Maybe you'd better enjoy it while you can and not complain."

Nodding, she concentrated on the road, but she could feel his gaze on her until she turned onto Catalina Highway and he fell into a fitful sleep.

Kathryn threw him an anxious glance when he twisted in his seat and threw one arm up over his eyes. He really was tired and he seemed to be too warm because he continually pulled at his shirt collar. Kathryn adjusted the air conditioner vent to blow directly on him and was glad when he calmed down.

Although she had been to his house once, it was hard to find in the dark. Finally she came to a stop in front of the house she had admired earlier that day, a rambling structure of Southwestern-style terra-cotta brick.

She reached over to touch Reid and was surprised at how warm he felt. "Reid. You're home."

Once again he came instantly awake. He ran a hand across his face and flexed his shoulders. "Thanks for picking me up."

Kathryn's lips curved at the soft tone of his voice. She stared at him anxiously for a moment, then handed him the keys and slid out, ready to go home.

Reid started to climb out of the Jeep, then hesitated, his feet almost on the ground, his eyes staring ahead at his home. "Are you hungry?" he called softly to her as she rounded the front of the Jeep.

"What?"

He pulled out his luggage and began unloading the boxed equipment. "Do you want to come in?"

# CHAPTER SEVEN

IN THE SOFT illumination of the dome light his face looked haggard. Kathryn thought he seemed almost wistful, too—completely at odds with his usual manner.

Her better judgment told her to go on home, but she wanted to be with him. "I'd like that," she said, reaching for his briefcase.

Carrying his luggage, he led the way to the double front doors. The solid cedarwood had weathered to a gray that was almost the color of Reid's eyes. When he unlocked the door and swung it open, Kathryn stepped inside and looked around eagerly at the inviting Southwestern-style decor.

The floor of the entryway was of gray stone. A bench that resembled an old church pew stood against one wall. Reid indicated she should set his briefcase on it and threw his jacket over the back. Carefully he brought in the rest of the equipment and stacked it out of the way.

Finished with that, he gave a quick, satisfied glance around at his home, signaling his pleasure in returning, and picked a packet of letters up from a small table. He flipped through them with one hand while he closed the door with his other.

Kathryn smiled at the casualness of the gesture. It was as if he was used to having her in his home.

The entryway opened into the living room where the predominant colors were those of the desert, from the gray of a dry river wash to the deep red of copper-filled hills. The furniture was big and comfortable without looking overstuffed.

The place was exactly as she would have expected. No fuss, no fripperies that would detract from his comfort or the basic practicality of his nature. She wondered fleetingly if his late wife had decorated it, but her mind refused to dwell on the thought. She was too caught up in absorbing the essence of Reid's home. There was nothing feminine about the place. It was purely Reid Darwin.

"Is something wrong?"

Reid's voice brought her back to reality. She looked up, blinking, embarrassed to be caught daydreaming. "No, not at all. You have a lovely home."

He looked around again, frowning slightly as if seeing it through her eyes. "Thanks," he said, treating her to one of his rare smiles. "Why don't you go into the den? I want to run up and check on Sean."

"Oh, may I come, too? He wasn't here when I came to pick up the Jeep," she asked quickly, earning a startled look. "I haven't seen him since the picnic," she finished lamely, then felt foolish for saying anything. Of course Reid would want some time alone with his son, even if the boy was asleep.

Reid surprised her with a quick, approving look. "Sure."

She followed him up the stairs, noticing how the soothing tones were carried through in the color scheme. On the second floor she glanced around at several doors and tried to decide which one led to Reid's bedroom and what it would look like inside. A king-size bed, no doubt, she thought, eyeing the big man beside her.

Reid opened a door and walked straight across to the dresser where he flipped the switch on a small box with a glowing red light.

"What's that?" she whispered.

"An intercom. Mother has one in her rooms on the other side of the house so she can hear Sean when I'm gone." Reid spoke in his normal tone of voice and Kathryn sent a startled glance toward Sean's bed before she remembered that the boy couldn't hear them.

She examined Sean's race car motif bedroom while Reid approached the bed, which was built like a Formula One racer, and looked down at his son. Kathryn was touched to see the flashlight she had given Sean lying on the bedside table.

In the glow from the hallway she could also see that the small pajama-clad figure didn't have a stitch of covers on. Reid bent and pulled the sheet up, then unself-consciously kissed Sean's plump cheek.

The tender gesture caught at her, twisting loose a warm, vital spurt of love for him. The feeling was so strong, she almost voiced it. Flustered, she stepped away and made a nervous circuit of the room, examining pictures and posters. When Reid checked the window lock, Kathryn took his place by the bed.

Sean was relaxed in a boneless sleep, his rounded cheek resting on his pillow.

Grinning, Kathryn turned away.

"What are you smiling about?"

"Even in sleep, he's an imp."

With a fond smile Reid nodded in agreement and led her back to the den. "I'll go find whatever food Mom left in the kitchen. Why don't you wait here?"

She nodded and sat on the plush couch by a fire-place made of rough desert rock. A tall arrangement of desert grasses in a terra-cotta jar stood on the hearth.

As soon as he left the room, her attention was caught by a large framed photograph on the coffee table. A blond woman holding a downy-haired baby smiled out at her, and Kathryn reached over and picked the picture up. Reid's wife, she thought, re-calling suddenly that Jill had said her name was Madeleine.

Comparing the two faces in the photo, she saw where Sean had inherited his wide, winsome smile. Again she felt an ache of regret at the way their fam-ily had been torn apart. If Reid's wife were still alive...

She couldn't say it was the wisest thing she had ever done, falling in love with this man, but she couldn't change it, even if she wanted to. In that instant she felt very alone.

At the sound of footsteps on the flagstone outside the door, Kathryn hurriedly set the picture down and leaned back, trying to compose herself.

"Roast beef sandwiches," he announced, pushing the door open and setting the covered tray down.

Kathryn lifted an eyebrow when he pulled the nap-kin off the tray. The sandwiches were thick and nu-merous enough to make a meal for an average-size family. His mother knew him well.

He had brought along a carton of milk and poured each of them a glassful.

"Maybe I should have made coffee," he said, frowning. "To keep you awake on the drive home."

"This is fine. Besides, you don't need anything that will keep you awake."

"I'm so tired, nothing could do that."

They ate in silence, and Kathryn noticed that for all his avowed hunger, Reid only finished one sandwich. He set his plate back on the tray and pushed his glass away, then settled himself against the back of the sofa.

Kathryn popped the last bite of sandwich into her mouth and looked up to see Reid rubbing the back of his neck. There was a pinched look around the corners of his eyes.

"Headache?"

His hand stilled and his eyes, smoky gray with fatigue, looked at her and then away. "It's all right."

Pride, she thought. He doesn't like to admit to human weakness. "I'll rub your neck for you."

"No."

"I used to do it for Maxie, one of the clowns I worked with. In fact, he was the one who taught me sign."

The exhausted lines of Reid's face shifted ever so slightly into a half smile. "Okay, please."

She stood and walked around to seat herself on the arm of the sofa. He leaned forward, pulled off his tie and undid the first couple of shirt buttons. His head tilted forward and he waited for her to begin.

Kathryn lifted her hands and stared at them for a moment. Though not small, they seemed woefully inadequate to relieve the tension that corded the back of his neck. She shook her head and placed her fingertips on his skin. With slow, circular motions she began to work out some of the stiffness she felt in him, and Reid showed his appreciation with a low-voiced grunt of satisfaction.

"Rough trip?" she asked, sliding her fingers up under the line of his tobacco-brown hair, working at the tight muscles.

"Pure hell."

She laughed softly at his aggrieved tone. "How was your presentation?"

"Okay, I guess. Started a lively discussion." Reid described the conversation that had gone on and she listened as her fingers continued their work.

As he talked she thought how right it felt to be alone with him like this, how very domestic. His usual brusqueness, his cautiousness were gone. And, given what she had discovered about herself this evening, so were hers. She had so many questions about him. Ones he might not be willing to answer.

Kathryn's eyes went to the twirling anniversary clock on the mantel. It was almost midnight, a time when barricades could easily fall. "Reid?"

"Hmm?" The lazy grunt made her wonder if he was half-asleep.

"I've been meaning to ask you, why did you waive the thirty-day review?"

His head turned and his brow furrowed. "Why are you asking now?"

She shrugged and dropped her hands into her lap. "I'm curious."

His eyes darkening in the lamplight, Reid watched her face for a few moments before he said, "Because you proved yourself. Are you finished rubbing my neck?"

Automatically her hands lifted once again to soothe and massage. Pleased with his answer, she wondered dreamily if she could ask him a few more things—such as what he thought of her. She felt his muscles finally beginning to relax, and Reid started talking in a quiet rumble about a new employee-incentive plan he had seen demonstrated.

Kathryn answered dreamily, only half listening. Her motion slowed, and her touch lightened until it was almost a caress.

The atmosphere of the room began to change. Solitude became intimacy, a caring gesture became a loving one.

Reid started to speak again but fell silent. Her hands went still and she waited, her fingers splayed over the cords of his neck, her heart quickening its beat.

One of his big square hands slipped up and trapped one of hers. Turning his head, he drew her hand down until the palm was even with his mouth. Eyes closed, he plunged his lips against her skin.

"Reid?" His name came from her throat in a little hiccup of surprised joy.

"I should have stopped you from rubbing my neck. It gives me ideas. Come here," he murmured, turning, sliding back, tumbling her into his lap. She fell willingly because her bones could no longer hold her.

One of his arms supported her back, the other formed an immovable band around her waist. His eyes were languorous, silver fire kindled in their depths. "I've been thinking about you all week."

She tilted her head back so that her coppery hair flowed in a cascade over his hand. "You—you have?"

"Yeah. Tuesday, when Sykes was trying to make a date with you, I wanted to do this—" his hand slid up to cup her chin, holding her still, so her eyes couldn't stray from his "—I wanted to kiss you."

She couldn't have torn her gaze from his, even though a moment of sanity tried to push itself into her consciousness. "It didn't seem to affect you very much the last time. You just walked away," she said, confused as much as she was excited.

He responded by slipping the fingers of his other hand deep into her hair until they cupped the back of her head.

Kathryn's eyes were wide with excitement and longing, her lips open as she tried to think of something to say. Reid took advantage of her involuntary acquiescence to lift her mouth to his.

It wasn't a chaste kiss but an exploring one, a burning, consuming one. He groaned low in his throat when she began to respond to him.

Excitement pounded through Kathryn, and she wound her arms around his neck, pulling herself as close as possible to him. A stream of fire seemed to flow through her from every place he touched.

There was no comfort to be found in this kiss, only raw need. Reid tasted and enticed her, his mouth scorching her until she was clasping his neck, bunching up the loosened collar of his shirt. Her fingertips ran over his skin, emulating the massage she had just given him, but with a much more selfish purpose. She wanted to touch him, to draw him to her.

In spite of her awareness of him and the emotions that had always simmered between them, Kathryn had tried never to imagine herself being with him like this. If she had, she knew now her imagination wouldn't have done justice to the truth of it.

"I didn't want this..." Reid murmured against her throat, his hands moving down her sides and settling on the lush curve of her hip, putting a lie to the very words he spoke. "I want you. I can't help myself."

"You can't?" She tilted her head, reveling in his hot, insistent mouth on her throat.

"No," he said gruffly, but he didn't stop kissing her—lips, eyes, the curve of her ear. "I've tried to keep away..."

"W-what do you mean?"

"I don't want—" he insisted, his words slurred.

Kathryn could feel his struggle. She plunged her hands into his hair and held his head still, kissing him with wanton abandon, desperate to not have the moment snatched from her. "What is it you don't want, Reid?"

His eyes were closed, his face contorted as his lips plundered hers. Breathing raggedly, he pulled away and buried his face against her neck. "This...you."

He held her still, his breath puffing against her skin for a moment, then he set her away from him suddenly and heaved himself up. Leaning forward, he dug his elbows into his knees and buried his face in his hands.

Breathless with the swift plunge from passion to withdrawal, Kathryn just stared at him. She made no move to straighten the dress that had ridden up her thighs or to smooth the wild mane of hair tangled around her face.

Although she steadied herself with a breath, her voice wavered. "What do you mean?"

Reid stood suddenly and prowled across to the mantel where he leaned his head on his hands. The big muscles in his shoulders bunched beneath the seams of his shirt, and Kathryn could see where her ravening hands had creased the fabric.

"I'm not ready to get involved again," he said, his voice low and ragged. "Not with...someone like you."

On shaky legs Kathryn stood up, belatedly making repairs to her clothes and hair. Why? The question came as a near scream within her. Because she was his secretary? Improper, of course. Impossible, maybe, but rules had been broken before. Why?

Her head lifted proudly, but she didn't say anything until he turned to look at her. When his dark gaze was on her face, she said, "Oh, I see" through a haze of humiliation and rejection.

Reid's eyes shifted from her, downward to the table by her knees. She glanced down, too, her gaze following his, until they were both looking at the same thing. The picture of Madeleine and Sean.

Her eyes flew to his face, noting the longing, regret and sorrow that etched his features. That's why he'd pulled back. He was still in love with his wife. Feeling utterly foolish and suddenly numb, Kathryn turned away.

"Good night," she said, as the hurt and confusion threatened to overwhelm her. Shakily she picked up her purse and walked to the door, anxious to get away, to try to deal with the rejection—to think.

He stayed by the mantel and made no move to stop her.

THE OLD STONE HOUSE was quiet when Kathryn came out of her room the next morning. Gratefully she saw that her roommates were gone. At least she wouldn't have to make awkward explanations about the circles under her eyes. She poured herself some coffee and winced at the way her hand shook.

Anybody viewing her would think she had gone a few rounds with a heavyweight boxer, but the bruises were on the inside.

She sat down at the kitchen table and stared at the Formica top.

Reid didn't want to get involved with a woman like her. What did that mean? A woman with red hair? she thought wildly. A secretary? Or just someone who wasn't Madeleine?

She rubbed her bare arms beneath her short-sleeved top. And she'd thought there was something about her he didn't like! No—he'd said she had proven herself. She'd have to face it. Love for his late wife and memories of their life together were the reasons he didn't want to get involved.

She could quit her job, run away from the hurt and the pain. Run away from him. But Jill was depending on her—so was Reid, for that matter.

Kathryn sipped her coffee, feeling the dubious benefits of the caffeine flowing into her system. It might be possible for her to continue working for Reid as long as she kept her distance and didn't let him know how much he meant to her. After all, he hadn't asked her to be foolish enough to fall in love with him.

The question was, did she have the strength to stay?

Sounds of feet scraping on the front porch and Bosco's joyous barking snagged her attention.

Seconds later Roxie bustled into the kitchen.

"Good morning," Roxie sang out. "A bit of a sleepyhead this morning, aren't you? Grandma's off at one of her cronies' houses, probably planning a sit-down strike at city hall." Roxie set a white bag down on the counter. "I ran over to the bakery and got some of their sinfully delicious pastry. It's guaranteed to bypass your digestive system and go straight to your hips." She looked up, her brown eyes shining with mischief. "Want some?"

"Sure, why not?" Kathryn took another sip of coffee and stood up to get a couple of plates and avoid Roxie's probing eyes.

"What's the matter with you? Are you sick? Because if you are, this pastry—"

Kathryn wheeled around to meet Roxie's sharp gaze. "I'm fine."

"Lying will make your nose grow. You want to look like Pinocchio?" Roxie brought the bag to the table, plopped into a chair and propped her feet up. "Tell me what's bothering you."

Because she needed to talk and because Roxie probably knew her better than she knew herself, Kathryn told her what had happened the night before.

Roxie examined a sweet roll, flaked off a bit of icing and let it melt in her mouth while she considered. "So, Iron Eyes doesn't want involvement, huh? He probably means romantic involvement."

Kathryn's green-gold eyes blinked at her. "Well, of course. Isn't that what we're talking about?"

"Not necessarily. There are all kinds of involvements... friendship, for instance."

"Do you think I could just be friends with him?"

Roxie shrugged, her shoulders lifting the straps of the baggy overalls she wore with a tank top. "The question is, do you think so? As I see it, you have to do what's best for yourself. You're in love with him— he doesn't want that. The next best thing is friendship, which he might want. Never know till you try."

Kathryn sat back, examining the suggestion. Was it possible she could stay and become Reid's friend? And not have to go away and never see him again? She couldn't lose any more than she already had. "I think you could be right."

"Of course I am," Roxie smirked. "Here, eat up. I don't want to be the only fat one in the house."

Still thoughtful, Kathryn complied.

She spent the day doing her Saturday housekeeping chores and practicing a couple of new magic tricks. Anything to keep herself busy. When the phone rang that evening and she picked up the receiver, Reid's was the last voice she expected to hear.

"Kathryn, is that you?"

Kathryn nearly dropped the glass from which she had been sipping iced tea. For all her fine resolve to keep things light and friendly, it was hard to hold her voice steady. "Yes, Reid, what is it?"

"I need you . . . well, I need Katydid the Clown." There was an edge to his voice that put Kathryn on the alert.

"Katydid!"

"Yeah, can you do it?"

"Do what?"

He sighed. "I'm sorry, I know I'm not making sense. Sean's sick with the flu, probably the same thing that's been going around the company. Anyway, he's asking for Katydid."

"Sean wants to see Katydid?"

"He's running a fever," Reid said, and just the sound of his voice lifted Kathryn's heart. "We've talked to the doctor, made him comfortable, but still he wants to see Katydid. If you're not afraid of catching this . . ."

"No, that doesn't worry me," she said hurriedly. She wasn't sure she was ready to see Reid again so soon, though. But friends, she told herself firmly, were to be counted on in times of trouble. "I'll be right over."

"Thank you. I'll tell him you're on your way."

Kathryn dashed for her room.

Roxie pounded along right behind her. "What are you going to do?"

In quick bursts of speech between putting on her wig and wriggling into her costume, Kathryn explained. "He needs me. Not Reid really—his son. Have you seen my greasepaint?"

"It's in your hand."

Kathryn looked down. You're too eager, she told herself. "Oh, of course. How stupid." She plunked herself down on the chair before her vanity and began applying it.

Roxie beamed at her like a proud mother whose child had taken its first unassisted steps. "Good girl. Remember to keep it friendly. My motto is that it's all right to chase a man as long as he doesn't know it."

Kathryn frowned at her. "Don't make too much of this. I'm just going to comfort a sick child."

"The question is, what do *you* make of it?" Roxie asked as she sashayed from the room.

"Good question," Kathryn muttered, grabbing up her purse and heading out to the old Buick.

Traffic was light and it didn't take her long to reach Reid's home. He was waiting on the front porch when she drove up and he hurried to open the car door for her.

"Kathryn, thank you for coming."

She could see the worry lines carved in his face that made him look haggard. Inside the house, he led her up to Sean's room.

Feverish eyes lit, Sean raised his hand to say hi. Kathryn rushed to his side and took the small hand in her own. "Hello, Sean," she said cheerily in her best Katydid voice as her fingers spoke to the boy. "Feeling pretty bad?"

He moaned and nodded.

Kathryn smoothed sweat-dampened blond hair from his forehead. "I'm glad your daddy called me. I'm working on a couple of new tricks and I need an audience—someone who can't run away if the tricks flop."

"I can't run," Sean signed, and there was a forlorn droop to his mouth. "My legs hurt."

"His fever's been pretty high," Reid said from behind her. "Mom's gone to the pharmacy to get something for it. I guess I could have gone, but . . ."

Mentally Kathryn finished the sentence for him. He couldn't bear to leave Sean. She glanced up at Reid's drawn face. He looked out on his feet.

"Why don't you go relax for a while? I'll stay with him." She indicated the big bag she had hurriedly stuffed. "I'll make him a couple of balloon animals. Maybe even try a race car," she signed, for Sean's benefit. Sean's mouth curved into a wan smile.

"All right. I'll be in the den." Reid left the door open behind him.

After unloading a few props, Kathryn made Sean a couple of balloon cars, inventing the designs as she went along. When they were done, he held them while she signed a simple, made-up story about two cars, best friends, who were entered in the same race. He drifted off to sleep before she could think of a satisfying ending to their dilemma.

Kathryn sat with him for a while to make sure he was deeply asleep, then packed her supplies and went downstairs. Reid was sprawled on the well-remembered couch in the den, a pot of coffee and a half-eaten sandwich near him on the table. Although the memories of the two of them together were vivid, Kathryn fought them down.

"Coffee this time of night?" She said the first thing that came to her.

Reid lifted his head from where it rested on the back of the sofa. He shook his head groggily. "I want to stay awake in case Sean needs me."

Firmly Kathryn took the pot and moved it out of reach. "It won't do either of you any good if you get sick, too."

He heaved himself to a sitting position and, propping his elbows on his knees, put his face in his hands. A deep sigh gusted from his lips as he ran his hands through his hair, leaving it spiked up around his head.

"No, I guess not, although I wonder if I could have brought this flu home to him."

"I doubt it. Sean came down with it too fast. But even so, you can't blame yourself."

One of Reid's bushy brows lifted. "Why not? I'm his father. There's no one else to blame."

"You can't protect your child from everything."

He ran his hands across his eyes. "I know—" his voice was rough and granitelike "—I couldn't even protect him from a cold when he was two, and he ended up deaf."

Kathryn sank into a chair. She had assumed that Sean had been born deaf. "A cold?"

"Yeah, it turned into meningitis. He almost lost his life. Somehow his hearing seemed a small price to pay when measured against that."

"One way or another, you've lost a lot, haven't you?"

He had been staring at the carpet beneath his feet. At her question his head rose slowly until his gray eyes were virtually piercing right through her. There was no mistaking the wariness in them. "You mean Madeleine?"

"Yes."

"She died two years ago—a car wreck."

"I know. It must have been terrible."

His big shoulders convulsed fractionally, then straightened. "It was. Needless to say, you probably think I'm overprotective where Sean is concerned. I guess I did overreact to this flu thing." His wide mouth curved in a rueful smile. "I hope you don't get it."

"I won't, but if you're worried about it, why did you suggest that I come over?"

Reid shrugged. "Sean likes you."

"And?"

His gray eyes studied her face. "I wanted to explain about last night."

# CHAPTER EIGHT

KATHRYN'S HANDS clasped together in front of her.
She might be about to hear something she would
rather not know. "Last night you said you didn't want
to get involved with someone like me. What did you
mean?"

Reid stabbed a hand through his hair. "Someone
who tries to fix things."

"Oh, we're back to that." Kathryn rolled her eyes
and turned, prepared to leave. Why didn't he just tell
her the truth and be done with it—tell her he couldn't
forget his wife and make room for another love?

Reid's forceful voice stopped her. "You have to
admit, you tend to do that. You jumped into Jill's job
so she wouldn't worry. You hired Roxie because she
couldn't seem to settle into a job. Shall I go on?" He
was watching her reaction carefully. "You and
me...together. It's just a bad idea."

Kathryn punched her fists onto her hips. "I also
rescue cats from storms and take in dogs no one else
wants. Not to mention comforting sick boys."

Reid lifted both thick eyebrows. "Touché."

"It's called friendship, Reid. It's called helping
make people's lives a little easier. You say people take
advantage of me, but I don't see it that way." Her
mind skipped back to his kisses of the night before and
stuck on the way he'd withdrawn from her and just

stared at the picture of his wife. "At least, I never used to," she added.

Palms out in a placating gesture, Reid said, "All right. Maybe we can just agree to disagree about exactly what it is you do, as long as you bear in mind that some things can't be fixed."

"So you've told me before." Kathryn clutched her prop bag. "Thanks for this enlightening little chat. I'll see you Monday." She glanced back over her shoulder to see him scowling at her. "I assume you don't mind if I stay on as your secretary."

"Wait." He dragged a hand over his haggard face. "Don't rush off before I finish."

Resolute, she turned back, her bag gripped in her fist. She wanted to be friends with him. Fat chance. He kept pushing her away. Worse, he couldn't accept her concern for others as part of her personality. "Go on."

Now that he had her full attention, Reid looked as if he wanted to choose his words carefully. He speared his fingers through his hair and sighed lustily. "I've let this drag on far too long—go too far—without explaining myself."

Kathryn shifted uncomfortably, wondering if he knew at all how easily he could hurt her. "What do you mean?"

"My...reaction to you..." He caught her level stare and said, "Bear with me for the moment. Anyway, there's more to it." He paused and took a deep breath, his big chest expanding for a moment as if he was drawing in understanding.

Kathryn had to admire him for finally being willing to talk about it, but it sure was taking him a long time to get to the point. Part of her wanted him to take forever. Part of her wanted to face the worst now. "Well?"

"Madeleine was always trying to fix things—specifically Sean's deafness."

The words came out in a flat rush, with no emotion behind them that Kathryn could decipher. She strained so hard to pick up hidden clues that she found she was holding her breath.

"She consulted one doctor after another, gathered information about treatments," he went on. "At one point I thought she was going to try a faith healer." Reid looked as if he wanted to say more, but he bit the words off, gave a slight shake of his head and gazed down at his hands.

Kathryn wondered if she should push him, ask questions, but it had taken him so long to tell her even this little bit, she was reluctant.

She tried to read the feelings that were now playing across his blunt features. She saw his gray eyes darken as they sought the picture on the table.

He had loved Madeleine in spite of her apparently misguided efforts to cure Sean's deafness. Kathryn felt that with all certainty. She placed her prop bag on a table by the door and ran her palms down the front of her ruffled costume skirt. All right, she could accept that—if only she could believe that eventually he could make room in his heart for her.

She was tempted to explain why she tried to make things easier for people, but she held back. It might sound foolish to him that a twenty-five-year-old woman could still be affected by events that had happened before she was ten.

Her voice was low and earnest when she spoke. "I'm sorry. It must have been difficult for both of you."

He lanced a steellike gaze at her. "To say the least."

Kathryn clasped her hands in front of her to prevent herself from going to him and enfolding him in her arms. "You have to admit my 'fix-it' projects are more practical, though," she said in a light tone that sounded just a bit forced.

"Kathryn..."

"But you don't want to get involved with me."

It took him a moment to answer and that gave her momentary hope.

"That's right," he said slowly.

Kathryn watched his face, wanting to know so much more about him, wanting to tell him more about her. It couldn't just end here, like this. Roxie's suggestion would have to work. It had to. "How about if we were just friends?"

"I beg your pardon?"

Pleased that she had caught him off guard, Kathryn smiled, stretching her huge Katydid grin even bigger, to take in a real smile of her own. "Friends. You know, those people who come over to your house and don't mind if you haven't mopped your floors in a month. People who ride in your car and don't mention the twelve crumpled fast-food restaurant bags under their seat."

A corner of Reid's mouth shifted upward. "You think *we* could be just friends?"

"Sure. Why not? We have a lot in common."

"Like what?"

Kathryn's mind blundered about. "We work for the same company!"

"I don't exactly work for it," he pointed out.

Kathryn waved that aside airily. "Your paycheck comes from the same place mine does. I've seen it."

"All right. I'll concede that. So what's your point?"

"I'll bet we have similar tastes in literature. Do you read the backs of cereal boxes?"

Reid's expression tilted into a full smile. "Sometimes."

"Music? I like anything that's played on wood, strings, brass or jukeboxes. How about you?"

"That covers a pretty broad territory."

"Do you put your pants on one leg at a time?"

"Every day." His chuckle sounded genuine, but Kathryn suspected he was relieved she hadn't asked more questions about Madeleine, just as she knew she was disappointed he hadn't offered more explanation.

She forged ahead, her green-gold eyes taking on a soft glow. "I like your son."

"So do I. What are you getting at?"

Kathryn took a deep breath and plunged on. "That you don't have to expect me to try and fix things for Sean—or you. Friends don't try to change each other. How about it?" She stuck out her hand. "Friends?"

One of Reid's massively powerful hands enveloped hers and squeezed gently. "It's hard to say no to a clown. Okay—friends."

Although tremors of awareness were shooting through her from where their hands were joined, Kathryn kept her smile in place. Love overflowed her heart, and she was grateful for the full clown makeup that hid her true thoughts. She prayed fervently that she wouldn't regret this. Friends, she reminded herself firmly. Just friends.

After a moment she drew her hand away and once again picked up her prop bag. "I'd better go. Let me know if Sean needs me again."

"I will. I think he's going to sleep for a while now." Reid led the way outside and held her car door open for her while she slipped inside, then slammed it shut behind her. "Be careful going home."

"I will," Kathryn said, smiling up at him. This conversation was an inane end to the events of the past two days, but she reminded herself that it was the kind of talk friends shared.

As she drove away, she watched Reid in her rear-view mirror. The sun was setting, sending glints of gold over his hair and highlighting his carved features. It must have been a trick of the setting sun because she thought she saw longing in his expression.

The memory stayed with her throughout the rest of the weekend, making her want more than she knew she was going to get. She pushed her wants aside and practiced friendly smiles, and when Reid walked into her office on Monday morning she had one all ready.

He seemed to be in a thoughtful mood as he thanked her again for coming to see Sean.

"I was glad to do it. How is he this morning?"

"His fever broke about midnight. He was sleeping soundly so I decided to come to work."

"I'm glad," she said breathlessly, aware that her face must be shining up at him. Friends, huh? From the way she was beaming, he would be tempted to run and lock himself in his office. Lowering her eyes, she began fumbling with some papers. "Because now you can help deal with all of last week's mail."

Reid winced comically. "I never suspected you had a mean streak in you."

Keep it light, she reminded herself. "I've only been showing you my better nature. Since we're friends, I can let you see the real me."

"I can't wait," he grumbled, taking the big stack and turning back to his own office.

Reid was closeted in meetings for the rest of the day, so Kathryn saw little of him. It was probably just as well, she thought, because she needed time to think about what had occurred over the weekend.

A few days later, she received a call from Jared Sykes who asked her out again. Without Reid breathing down her neck to unnerve her, Kathryn turned him down firmly, though she hated to hurt his feelings.

After she hung up, she wondered how many more men she would refuse to date because she and Reid were "just friends." She almost laughed. Who would have thought she would get herself into such a situation?

Chin in hand, she sat and pondered the dilemma until she heard people calling good-night to each other. With a start, she realized most of the other employees had left. She stood and started into the hall to see if Reid needed anything before she went home. She knew he planned to work late going over the new employee incentive program he and the personnel department had developed.

She was just about to step into Reid's office when the outside door at the end of the hall opened and Sean Darwin rushed in followed by his grandmother.

Kathryn's gaze tracked the little boy fondly. He looked completely well again.

Sean emitted one of his endearing squeaks and launched himself at his father.

"Grandma's going to take me to McDonald's for a hamburger." Sean cupped his hands lightly and patted them together to indicate his favorite food. "My tummy's all better."

"I decided some junk food would be just the thing to fix him up," Mrs. Darwin said, strolling up behind her grandson.

"I'm glad you brought him in since I'll be here late tonight." Reid held the door open for his mother. The three of them went inside and Kathryn returned to her own office.

Clearing her desk took far longer than Kathryn had expected. She was hastily prioritizing her work for the next day when she saw a movement out of the corner of her eye. Sean was standing there, grinning shyly. Voices in the hall told her Reid and his mother were outside his office once again, talking.

"Hello, Sean," she signed. "I'm Kathryn."

He mimicked her, forming the letter K by her curly red hair to indicate that was how he would remember her. He glanced around her office and his face brightened when he saw her computer. "Can I play?"

She explained that the computer was a tool, not a toy, but she let him sit in her chair, got out a graphics program and knelt to show him how to use it for drawing. He was enthralled and treated her to smiles and sideways glances.

Kathryn returned his smile in bemusement. Why, the little stinker was flirting with her! And he didn't even know that they had met before. What a heartbreaker!

They talked and played for several minutes and she caught Sean staring at her hands with interest even when she wasn't signing.

"Do you know Katydid?" he asked, turning his melting blue eyes up to her.

"I am Katydid," she said, surprised that he seemed able to recognize a person's hands as she would know someone by their voice.

Sean studied her face and her nose, then glanced at her hair. "No way," he signed, bursting into his chortling laugh.

Kathryn couldn't resist squeezing him. "It's true. I dress up in a costume and put on makeup to be Katydid. All clowns are just regular people, too."

He looked skeptical. "You mean you're two people?"

Again Kathryn laughed and ran her finger down his soft cheek. "Yes, I am."

"I knew you were Katydid, anyway," he said with a superior look.

"Oh, really?"

"Yeah, you smell good. Just like her. Besides, you like to hug me," he added with a grimace of long-suffering patience.

Kathryn surrendered her heart without a fight. Leaning over, she kissed his cheek, but he slid from the chair and danced away from her, his sweet little features screwed up. "Oh, that's mean," he said, shaping both hands into claws, then into the letter A, and scraping his knuckles together. He wiped vigorously at his cheek.

Kathryn held her nose. "Well, you little stinker!" Laughing, she lifted her head to see Reid and his mother standing in the doorway. Mrs. Darwin's face was affectionately indulgent. Reid was watching them intently and she wondered what he was thinking.

Self-consciously, she stood, brushed off her skirt and smiled at Mrs. Darwin who greeted her warmly. Sean danced over to grab his grandmother's hand and drag her toward the door, anxious for his dinner at McDonald's. Reminded of his manners, he stopped long enough to say goodbye to Kathryn and kiss his father.

As the door swung shut behind the two of them, Kathryn shared a smile with Reid. "He's really something," she said.

"Yeah." Reid's voice rang with pride. "Are you leaving?"

"As soon as I clear my desk." She started to turn away, but he stayed where he was, watching her. He had discarded his suit jacket, loosened his tie and rolled up his sleeves sometime during the afternoon. The casualness made him look virile and desirable. When his gaze touched her face, Kathryn felt an odd little kick in her heart. "Did you need something?" she asked.

He blinked and shook his head. "No. Good night." He headed back to his office, and thoughtfully, she returned to her desk.

She was almost out the door when the purchasing manager dashed up with some bid papers that needed to be typed. Because the bid had to be hand-delivered by nine o'clock the next morning, Kathryn bit back her reluctance and agreed to do it. She closed her office door to ensure solitude from the departing employees.

Typing bids was her least favorite job because of the attention to detail that was required. A misplaced decimal point could mean disqualification of the bid. When the papers were finally finished and proofread, she glanced up to see that it was almost seven o'clock. Her empty stomach reminded her that she had eaten lunch on the run and skipped dinner altogether. She rolled her shoulders, which were knotted from bending over the typewriter, and stood up, intending to carry the bid to the purchasing office on her way to the parking lot.

Kathryn tucked her purse under her arm, picked up the bid and flipped off the light. She stepped out into the dark hall but had taken only two steps when she was grabbed from behind.

She shrieked and was immediately freed.

"Kathryn!" Reid's shocked voice spoke in the darkness. "I'm sorry. I thought you'd gone home hours ago. I was just on my way out and saw the light go off in your office." As he spoke, his hands lightly cupped her shoulders to steady her.

Kathryn was trying hard to swallow her heart, which felt as if it had leaped into her throat. Gasping, she said, "I could have been one of the warehouse crew, you know."

"Except they never come to this part of the building." Reid's big hands massaged her shoulders.

Tilting her head back Kathryn squinted to see his face in the darkness. At that moment the dim hall lights, controlled by a timer, clicked on. She blinked owlishly.

"Are you all right? I didn't mean to scare you." Gruff tenderness sounded in his voice.

The hand that had flown toward her throat still covered her pounding heart, but she nodded. "I'm fine, but please don't ever do that again. For a second there I thought Rambo was in the building." She wished she could melt against him and be comforted forever.

Reid offered a relieved smile. "Not Rambo. Just the company president jumping on unsuspecting employees. What are you doing here so late, anyway?"

Kathryn explained as she tried to smooth out the wrinkles her clutching fingers had made in her clothes when Reid grabbed her. "I was just on my way to put the bid on the purchasing manager's desk before heading home."

Nodding, he stepped back. "I see. Well, I'll get out of your way, then."

"Good night." She turned away and was several yards down the hall when he caught up to her. With an amused glance, she turned to him. "Keeping an eye on me? Don't worry. There's no one else around to mistake me for a burglar."

"You'll probably never let me forget that. Why don't you let me make it up to you?"

She swept into the purchasing department, dropped off the bid and came back to him, smiling impishly. "You're afraid I'm going to put this in the company newsletter, aren't you?"

He grinned, wiping tired lines from his face and adding a hint of merriment to his eyes. "I figure I'd better offer you a bribe."

Kathryn started for the parking lot and he fell into step beside her. "Like what?"

"Have you had dinner?"

"No. I was going home to raid the refrigerator." She stopped by her car and smiled up at him. "Of course, at my house there's always the chance that Wilma has had a dozen friends in and the cupboards are bare.

They seem to think the way to save the world is to eat up every scrap of food.''

Reid chuckled, and Kathryn reveled in the easy, relaxed sound. "Then let me buy you dinner. It's the least I can do after scaring you out of your wits."

"So now you're saying I'm witless."

He smiled, waiting for her answer. She hesitated. Going out to dinner with him wasn't any way to stay uninvolved. He obviously knew that, too. On the other hand, it was the kind of thing friends did all the time. "All right, Reid. I'd like that."

"Great." He rubbed his hands together. "How do you feel about green corn tamales?"

"Greedy."

"Follow me, then." Reid held the door for her, locked the building, climbed into his Jeep Cherokee, and waited for Kathryn to pull out in her car and trail him. Within a few minutes they were at a busy restaurant on Tucson's east side. Reid secured a table and ordered drinks, which came with a basket of warm tortilla chips and salsa hot enough to melt paint off a barn.

Unsuspecting, Kathryn had taken one bite before diving for her glass of ice water, downing it in one gulp. She came up gasping, wheezing, and watery-eyed. "That stuff's lethal!"

Reid loaded a chip with the tomato and pepper mixture and popped it into his mouth. "Don't be a sissy. I thought you were a native Arizonan."

"I am, but I'm not crazy." She gave him a narrow glance. "Next you'll tell me it'll grow hair on my chest." Her face reddened when she realized what she had said, but Reid's amused gaze didn't lower by even a fraction of an inch.

"Your chest is fine as it is," he said and signaled the waitress to take their orders.

Grateful that he was willing to overlook her remark and chiding herself for not keeping any hint of sexual talk out of their conversation, Kathryn launched into news about the company. They drifted into exchanges about their childhoods and Kathryn was delighted to learn they had many similar interests. She was surprised to find that he planned to sign Sean up for Little League the next spring.

"Do you think that's wise?" she asked, taking a bite of savory rice.

Reid looked up, eyebrows raised. "Sure. Why not? He's a natural."

Spoken like a proud father, Kathryn thought, but she didn't mention the obvious reason—Sean's deafness. She didn't want him to think she was interfering. True friends understood and supported. They didn't meddle. If she told herself things like that often enough, she might come to believe them.

Reid and Kathryn moved on to other topics, talking easily about a variety of subjects. If Kathryn hadn't already loved him, she would have come to do so that evening. He was more open with her than he had ever been.

As they lingered over coffee, Kathryn experienced an odd feeling of disappointment. Reid was able to relax with her now as he never had before, but his treatment of her was much like his attitude toward Jill, or Lydia Martinez or any other woman in the company.

Kathryn looked down at the dark brew into which she had swirled cream. She and Reid were nearly friends now, and at her suggestion. He could relax because he had laid everything on the line and told her he wouldn't become involved with her. Kathryn couldn't help longing for the kind of intimacy they had enjoyed on the couch in his den before he had pulled back from her, remembering his wife and closing Kathryn off.

Reid was safe now, while Kathryn felt like a child who had been climbing for the cookie jar only to have her supporting chair kicked from beneath her.

# CHAPTER NINE

As LONG AS she didn't probe beneath the surface, Kathryn thought the friendship between herself and Reid might work. If she didn't consider what could have been or what she wanted from him, she could coast along.

Having dinner together when they both worked late became an occasional event. They even went to a couple of movies together, and it amused her to discover he liked spy movies and thrillers.

Somehow she and Reid did manage to become friends of a sort despite their opposite views of life— her optimism and his caution, her searches behind clouds for silver linings and his pragmatism.

One weekend they explored the foothills of the Catalina Mountains and took Sean to the Arizona Sonora Desert Museum. He loved the twelve-acre park with its displays of desert wildlife in natural settings.

Slowly Kathryn learned things about Reid, although he always maintained a distance Kathryn found disturbing. Once he mentioned his father who had died soon after Sean's birth. Reid had tremendous love and respect for his father, who had never been too busy working to play catch with his only son. She began to understand why Reid was such a good father.

He never talked about Madeleine, though, and Kathryn couldn't help but think he was still in love with his late wife and grieving for her.

Reid had to make another trip to Phoenix, and on the afternoon he was gone, while Reid's mother was busy with her bridge group, she picked Sean up and took him to her house where Wilma taught him to walk on his hands and had Bosco show off his tricks. That the tricks usually went awry didn't bother Sean at all. He chortled and shrieked with delight whether Bosco's performance was successful or not.

To Kathryn's mind Sean was everything a little boy should be, despite his handicap. He was bright and mischievous, with a huge capacity for love. She knew he had learned that love from his father—and she took heart.

One Saturday afternoon, Kathryn accompanied Reid and Sean to Old Fort Lowell Park. Since it was late September the weather had begun to cool a bit and they could stay outdoors comfortably most of the afternoon. Many other people had the same idea, and the park was crowded with picnickers.

The three of them admired the fenced-in remains of the adobe structure that had housed the U.S. Cavalry assigned to help keep peace in the Arizona Territory in the previous century. Sean signed endless questions asking how the adobe bricks were made, how old the fort was, and why it was all broken down, until finally Reid clapped his hand around the boy's flying fingers.

He picked his son up, threw him across his massive shoulder and dashed across the parking lot to a man-made lake. Sean whooped with laughter while Kath-

ryn ran along beside them. Reid threatened to dump
the boy in the lake if he asked one more question.

Sean read his father's signs, his little face solemn,
then asked impishly, "Can I go to the bathroom?"

Reid stamped his foot in a threatening way, and
Sean scampered away to the nearby rest room. When
Kathryn started to follow, the little boy looked back
huffily and signaled to her, "I don't need help!"

Bowing apologetically, Kathryn stopped and let him
proceed alone. "I was just going to wait outside the
door for him," she said.

Reid came up behind her and laid his hand on her
shoulder. "Don't be too protective, Kathryn. He's just
learning independence."

Resisting the urge to rest her cheek against his hand,
Kathryn turned puzzled green eyes to him. "Just
learning? I thought he was always like this. He doesn't
seem to be afraid of anything."

"No, not now..." His voice trailed off and he tilted
his head slightly, gazing at Kathryn with an odd light
in his eyes, as if he'd just remembered something.

With a half laugh of surprise, Kathryn asked,
"What's wrong?"

Reid didn't answer for a minute, then shook his
head, drew his hand away and continued. "When
Madeleine was desperate for a cure for Sean, he sensed
the tension between us and wanted one or the other of
us to always be around. When she and I were together, all we seemed to do was fight."

Kathryn shuddered, remembering what parents
fighting could do to a child. "I'm sorry, Reid. You
never told me."

His gray eyes flashed to her face, and she reminded
herself that there were dozens of things he hadn't told

her. Wondering at the odd look that had just passed over his features, she warned herself not to push for more. She turned away to look for Sean, who was coming toward them at a run, his shirt flapping outside of his shorts.

Laughing, Kathryn waylaid him and tucked his shirt in. He barely noticed, his attention was so caught by a couple of teenage boys prancing across the grass, bouncing soccer balls from one knee to the other.

"I wish I could do that," he signed.

"It takes practice," Reid answered, as he started to stroll slowly around the lakeside.

"Everything does." Sean shrugged and followed his dad, then gave Kathryn one of his flirtatious glances from beneath lowered lids. "That's what you said about juggling. I liked it when you showed me how to juggle."

"I'm glad." Kathryn strode easily along but clasped her hands at her sides so she wouldn't give in to the urge to grab Sean and kiss him. When he smiled he looked so much like Reid it made her heart ache.

"I liked it when you did magic tricks, too."

"Oh, really?" she said, charmed by the not-so-subtle way he was working up to his true goal.

"Yeah. Can you show me how to do magic?" he asked, circling with his fingers together, then opening his hands wide.

"What's this about magic?" Reid asked, glancing down sharply to catch the last word.

Sean explained in his rapid sign language, watching his father's face expectantly.

"That . . . sounds like fun."

Kathryn heard the hesitation in his voice, but she spoke up eagerly. "I'd love to do it."

Reid's gaze shifted to her as he signed to Sean. "I'm sure Kathryn would be too busy."

"Not at all," Kathryn said, exchanging delighted grins with Sean. "And he'll be a great student. Also, it helps me learn if I have someone to practice with." Unthinking, she laid a hand on Reid's hard forearm, and a muscle jerked under her fingers. "Remember how quickly Sean caught on to juggling?" she went on. "He seems to have a real talent for this kind of thing." She offered her most winning smile. "Besides, if you plan to sign him up for Little League, the kind of eye-hand coordination he can learn in magic will help in baseball." She glanced at Reid. At the look on his face, she was struck by disappointment.

"Sounds good, Sean." His hands were animated, but his face was a hard mask. "Maybe you can do it someday. Now why don't you feed the ducks?"

"When?" Sean wanted to know.

"Right now. We've got some bread crumbs in the Jeep."

"No, no. When can Kathryn show me how to do magic?"

Reid flicked a glance at her. "We'll decide later...."

Kathryn dug her hands into the pockets of her loose cotton slacks. Maybe this wasn't such a great idea. The signals Reid was sending told her to back off, but Sean was bouncing with joyful anticipation. She took a breath. "Tomorrow's Sunday, and I don't have a clowning job...."

"All right—" Reid finally said, raising his hands in a dismissive gesture. He didn't look happy. "Kathryn can come over tomorrow."

Sean agreed, grinning with excitement as Reid shepherded him around the rest of the lake, and Kathryn followed, deep in thought.

When they had finished their walk, Reid went back to the car for a bag of bread crumbs. Sean took it and began walking around the edge of the pond, dropping tantalizing bits of bread for the greedy ducks who followed him, quacking and complaining.

Reid sat down at the base of a tree, Kathryn a few feet away. He hooked his hands around one knee as he stared off toward the Catalina Mountains. His forehead was wrinkled as if he was deep in thought. Nearby a bunch of teenagers were playing Frisbee with a golden retriever.

"Do you see that development up there?"

Kathryn glanced at the red-roofed houses that she knew had been built on a blasted-out section, creating what most Tucson residents considered an eyesore.

"Yes."

"There used to be a road near there," he went on, the timbre of his voice dreamily low. "A sort of lover's lane."

Kathryn's head snapped around, sending red tendrils of her hair flying. "Oh?"

He hardly seemed to hear her response. "That's where I proposed to Madeleine. Seems so long ago."

Kathryn opened and closed her mouth a couple of times, trying to think of something to say. Why was he talking about this now? Kathryn tried to turn her thoughts with his, following the events of the past few minutes. Did he really think talking about his late wife wouldn't hurt Kathryn just because he'd no intention of becoming romantically involved with her?

Hovering between hurt and anger she was trying to form a reply when shouts startled them.

They looked up to see the Frisbee-playing retriever rounding the end of the lake in a flat-out race to catch the white disk that was floating farther and farther away.

Belatedly, the kids playing saw Sean meandering along, throwing out crumbs to the ducks, who waddled and paddled along behind and beside him.

Of course, the shouts went unheard.

Reid and Kathryn scrambled to their feet and started to run. Before they had taken two steps, the Frisbee whacked Sean on the back of the head, and the dog, unable to stop his forward momentum, crashed into Sean, sending the boy headlong into the pond.

Though the ducks flapped their wings to fly away for a moment, they were quickly back, greedily moving in to peck at the crumbs clinging wetly to Sean's hand. The frightened boy tried to get away, but he was impeded by the ducks, the water and the flailing dog.

Since they'd had a head start, the Frisbee players reached Sean first. They pulled him, shrieking, from the pond and collared their dog. When Reid rushed up, he practically threw the kids aside in order to reach his son.

Kathryn was right behind him, jerking off the loose cotton top she had over her T-shirt.

"Why didn't the kid get out of the way?" one of the boys muttered, looking at the muddy mess Sean was.

"Because he's deaf!" Kathryn snapped, shoving past the teenagers. "He couldn't hear you."

The kids fell back, apologizing.

Unmindful of the mud, Reid and Kathryn dropped to their knees beside the little boy. While he sobbed, she used her shirt as a towel to wipe off the muck that covered him, all the while signing words of comfort and love.

Reid muttered under his breath as he pulled Sean's shirt off and dropped it on the grass. "Damned careless kids. They could have watched what they were doing."

Behind them one of the teens spoke up hesitantly. "Lady, is your little boy okay?"

She glanced over her shoulder and offered a reassuring smile. "He'll be fine."

"She's *not* his mother." Reid's answer overrode hers.

Kathryn's eyes widened and shot to his grim face.

Reid stood and picked up Sean. "Come on, we'll take Kathryn home, then I've got to get you into some dry clothes."

She knew she should point out that he was overreacting. All little boys fell and got wet, but she knew he wouldn't want to hear it. She wasn't Sean's mother.

Besides, she wanted to get home. Reid's sudden snappishness had her completely confused. Somehow the tone of their friendship had changed this afternoon, and she needed to figure out why. Almost stumbling in her pain, she followed.

Over Sean's protests Reid bundled him into the car and held the door for Kathryn. All the way to her house he kept a fierce frown on his face and his jaw set. He hardly spoke until he pulled into her driveway. "We'll see you tomorrow."

Mystified, she turned to him. "Do you want to?"

His answer gusted out on a sigh that puzzled her even more. "Yes, yes, I want to." He reached up and

pinched the bridge of his nose as if he had the begin-
nings of a headache.

Sean shot forward to remind her she was supposed
to teach him magic. Nodding, she slid out of the car,
shut the door and watched as Reid reversed the car out
of the drive and sped away down the street.

Slowly Kathryn pulled herself out of her daze and
went into the house. It was blessedly quiet, so she
knew both her roommates were gone. She decided it
was just as well when she walked into her room and
looked in the mirror. Roxie and Wilma both would
have been on her immediately, trying to find out why
she looked so pale and shell-shocked.

She sat on the side of her bed and stared down at her
hands. Something was wrong—very wrong. She had
only been deluding herself, thinking she and Reid
could be friends, let alone anything more. No woman
would take Madeleine's place in his life or in Sean's.

Kathryn lay across her bed and threw an arm up to
shield her eyes, which were stinging with tears. In spite
of her promise to Jill, she was becoming convinced she
couldn't stay at TJS. Being near Reid hurt too much.

WHEN KATHRYN rang the Darwins' doorbell the next
day, her arms were loaded with her canvas prop bag
full of items for Sean's magic lesson. She had French-
braided her unruly hair so that it would be out of her
way and dressed in loose white slacks and top for ease
of movement.

During a troubled night of little sleep—not the first
she had spent since meeting Reid Darwin—she had
decided she would try to act as normal as possible for
Sean's sake. She was going to insist on talking to Reid
alone, although she didn't know what she intended to

say. He certainly hadn't invited her to fall in love with him.

Reid opened the door and Kathryn's green-gold eyes surveyed him over the top of her bag. She wondered why he looked as if his night had been as rough as hers. "Hello," she said cautiously. "Is Sean all ready for the lesson?"

He took the bag from her and studied her with a long, slow look before he answered. "Sean's practically bouncing off the walls."

Although tension started to twist her stomach, Kathryn stepped inside nonchalantly and dropped her purse on the old church pew in the entryway. "Good. I like enthusiastic pupils. Where shall we work?"

Reid closed the door. "The den?"

"No. I have visions of broken furniture." Not to mention her reluctance to see the picture of Madeleine that sat on the coffee table. "How about the patio?"

"Okay."

At that moment Sean bounded down the stairs and scampered to her. "Hi. I'm ready."

Kathryn smiled and followed him outside. When she had him settled practicing coin-palming and card tricks, she turned to Reid. "Your turn."

Somehow she wanted to get through to him, find out what he was thinking behind those enigmatic gray eyes—be close to him.

"Me?" Reid's brows shot up until they almost disappeared in his hairline.

"You're a natural. You juggle appointments all day. Here." She gave him the feather duster that could be transformed into a flower bouquet. "This is my simplest trick. I'm sure you can handle it."

Apparently he heard the desperate challenge in her voice. His head snapped up and his eyes narrowed on her. "Your faith in me leaves me speechless." Looking dubious, Reid took the stick of feathers and flipped the mechanism that made the flowers appear. A small smile worked its way into his features.

"Don't forget, there's more to it. You have to tell a story with your body and movements." She demonstrated, miming for him. He copied her and Kathryn watched, surprised that he would try at her request, but he was a little stiff.

She walked up to him, hesitating before lifting her hands. Would he jerk away from her touch? It would hurt if he did, but there was only one way to find out. She grabbed his shoulders, digging in with her fingers. "Loosen up," she said, giving him a slight shake. "This is just for fun, remember? Do it for Sean." She nodded toward the little boy who was ignoring them both.

"Fun. Right. You think that's what I need in my life?"

Kathryn's hands were still on his shoulders. She tilted her head back to look at his blunt, shuttered features. The bulky shoulder muscles bunched under her hands as she gazed at him, trying to say with her expression what she couldn't speak aloud. "I think you need—" she almost said "me" but swallowed it back and, flustered, turned away "—to have fun," she finished.

Wondering why she kept loving him when he wanted nothing from her, she began rustling in her bag for the colored handkerchiefs she was using in a new "disappearing ball" trick she was perfecting.

Sean and Reid soon gave up their efforts and sat down to watch her. They clapped when she did the trick successfully two times. Soon afterwards, Mrs. Darwin came out with a tray of cookies and lemonade. Sean virtually fell on the snack as if he had been wandering in the desert for days living on prickly pear fruit and barrel cactus water.

He stuffed cookies into his mouth with one hand and told Mrs. Darwin about his neat new card tricks with the other hand. His grandmother clucked over his manners and reminded him to share with the adults. When he finished his cookies, he wiped his mouth with the back of his hand, thanked Kathryn for the magic lesson and rushed into the house to play.

Kathryn joined Mrs. Darwin at a nearby round table shaded by an umbrella to enjoy the cooling afternoon. Reid lay stretched out on an oversize redwood chaise lounge that barely accommodated his length. His face was in shadow, while the sun glinted off the swimming pool and into Kathryn's eyes. She wished she could read his expression.

"I was watching you from inside, Kathryn. You really have quite a talent," Mrs. Darwin said, handing her a frosty glass of lemonade. "Do you ever miss the circus?"

"Oh, yes," Kathryn smiled, remembering. "Often. I loved it."

"Would you go back to it?"

Automatically Kathryn's gaze darted to Reid. She thought of the relatively uncomplicated life she had led in the circus and compared it to the tangle of emotions she found herself in with Reid. She had lost one love and never got to first base with the other.

"Sometimes I think I would. After all, it was my first love, and it's what I do best."

Mrs. Darwin looked surprised. "Then why did you leave the circus?"

Kathryn explained about the bankrupt Holley Brothers and the lack of openings with the bigger circuses. "Maybe if a position opened up and my qualifications were right, I would consider it." She nodded toward her prop bag. "I'm continually developing new tricks. A job for me? Who knows... Stranger things have happened—" Her voice choked and she cleared her throat. She wasn't even sure she meant what she'd just said. Leaving the company—leaving Reid—would be so darn difficult.

Mrs. Darwin laughed softly. "Reid, you'd better watch your p's and q's, then."

He didn't answer, and at that moment Sean came to the door and signed for his grandmother to come in the house. Excusing herself, she went with him and closed the sliding glass door behind her. Reid and Kathryn were left alone in the gathering dusk.

Kathryn sipped her lemonade carefully as the silence lengthened.

"What about your job?" Reid finally asked, and Kathryn twisted in her chair to see his face more clearly. Before she could answer, he sat up, then rose, looming over her. His eyes were piercingly direct. "If a clowning opportunity opened up, would you leave the company?"

"I guess I'd have to think about it." She rose to her feet, her chin lifted in challenge.

He snorted derisively. "You know, I've been thinking about what will happen when Jill comes back."

"What do you mean?"

"When she returns will you be happy to be just a junior secretary, I wonder? Or would you want to move on to another executive secretary position? Or go after a clowning job?" He fired the questions at her, one after the other. "After all, you might have a better chance now. You're good—I'll give you that, and you've developed new routines since you left the circus."

Chilled by his tone, Kathryn asked, "Would you even care if I left?"

"Of course," he said, but the look he gave her was harshly impersonal. "I wouldn't want to be left in the lurch."

Kathryn stared at him. He meant it. He really meant it. She was no more to him than an employee.

"I would never leave without giving proper notice and without training someone to take my place." Well what had she expected, anyway? He had been very precise about not wanting to get involved with her. She'd been the foolish one. After yesterday—his talk about Madeleine, his insistence that she wasn't Sean's mother—she should have known things wouldn't change.

She turned away from him and began stuffing articles into her canvas prop bag.

"What are you doing?"

"Going home."

He grabbed her wrist, forcing her to drop the deck of cards Sean had been practicing with. It fell at their feet. The box popped open and the cards scattered. She bent to pick them up, but he held her firmly. "Leave them."

"I've got to pick them up, Reid," she said through her teeth. "Or they won't be usable the next time Sean wants a lesson."

"There won't be a next lesson," he answered just as tightly, his gray eyes glittering.

"What?"

"Sean's lost enough in his life. I can't allow him to get too involved with someone who'll only be in his life a short time."

"I didn't say I would be leaving..." Kathryn began, then her words trailed off as she glared up into his tight face. Suddenly she knew what he was saying. She would never be anything but temporary to him or to Sean. That's what all the recent talk had been leading up to.

Reid acted as if he hadn't even heard her. "I was wrong," he said. "I thought a friendship between us would work. I thought I could let you into my life and my son's life—but I was wrong."

Kathryn stared at his angry, closed expression. If she had held any doubts about his determination not to love her, they had just been dispelled. There would never be a place in his heart for her. She had been pounding on a locked door.

With dignity she drew the strap of her bag over her shoulder and opened the sliding door. "Since I can't seem to change your mind—about anything—I'll go. Goodbye, Reid."

She slipped through the door and hurried across the living room, grateful she didn't meet Sean or Mrs. Darwin on her way out. She was in the entryway when Reid's voice reached her.

"Wait, Kathryn—don't leave like this when you're upset!"

Her pale face was as still as marble. Without bothering to answer, she swept the front door open and ran outside to the familiar old Buick. When she was in her car, she looked back to see Reid at the front door, his hands spread to grip both sides of the door facing. His brows were drawn together in a flat slash and his head was thrust forward.

She couldn't imagine why he'd try to stop her. He was so anxious for her to leave, anyway. Leave she would, and not just his home. There was no way she could stay on at Tucson Janitorial, breaking her heart over a man who didn't love her back. She had been a fool to stay as long as she had.

She kept her chin high as she started her car and drove off, but she had gone less than half a mile before she had to pull onto a quiet side street and give way to a storm of weeping.

She couldn't have said how long she sat there, but she cried until her head pounded and her eyes were swollen almost shut. Finally she wiped her eyes on the last tissue in her little purse packet and dropped it onto the floor littered with a dozen of its crumpled mates.

Shivering with reaction despite the heat, she started the car again and drove slowly home.

# CHAPTER TEN

DARKNESS CLOAKED the desert landscape by the time Kathryn got to her house. Her movements were slow as she gathered her props off the car seat. She felt as if she had run a marathon and fallen on her face just before the finish line. All her energy had been used up and she could barely make herself function. By the time she had pulled herself from the car and reached the porch, Roxie appeared in the doorway of the house and all but jerked her inside.

"Kath, what's going on?" she asked, her brown eyes brimming with concern.

Kathryn drew herself up, trying to hold on to her dignity despite the redness that puffed her eyes. "Wrong? Nothing."

"Nothing! Reid's been calling—"

"Reid?"

"Yes. He said he wanted to be sure you got home okay." She reached up to push Kathryn's hair off her face tenderly. "You should have heard him when I told him you weren't home. He was frantic!" Roxie shut the door and stood with her hands on her hips. "I'm supposed to call him as soon as you get here."

If it had been any other man, Kathryn would have thought his phone call meant he cared. But with Reid she knew better. "So call him," she said, letting her shoulders droop with exhaustion as she started for her room.

"Hey," Roxie asked. "Did you two have a fight?"

Kathryn shuddered. "I don't want to talk now, Rox." She kept moving inside her cocoon of numbness. "I just need to be alone. I'll see you in the morning."

Leaving her roommate muttering under her breath, she went into her room and shut the door, then walked straight toward the bathroom, stripping off her clothes as she went. Standing under the shower spray she let the cool water sluice over her. She wished it could wash away her thoughts, memories and regrets.

There was no point in staying at Tucson Janitorial, she decided, letting the spray hit her full in the face. Reid expected her to leave, anyway. She might as well fulfill his expectations. Tomorrow she would go to work early and type up a letter of resignation, effective immediately. Her assistant, Brianna, could handle a large share of the work until Reid found someone else.

Thinking of him, pain twisted inside Kathryn and she reached up to turn off the shower. Everything he had thought about her would be confirmed—that she was incompetent enough to leave him in the lurch, that she was flighty, that she certainly wasn't good enough...

Oh, what was the use? Viciously, she twisted the water faucet to the Off position, jerked back the shower curtain and stepped onto the mat. Going over it would change nothing.

The real reason for her departure might never occur to him, and she certainly wouldn't tell him now that she loved him.

ENDING HER ASSOCIATION with Tucson Janitorial Supplies took less than twenty minutes the next morning.

After a sleepless night she arrived at work before anyone else, typed up her resignation and left it on Reid's desk. She didn't allow her eyes to stray around the office in which they had worked so closely together. She hurried away. With one final glance at her own office she picked up the box of her personal belongings and dashed out.

Except for Bosco, who whined in excitement, and Hellion, who attacked her shoes as usual, her house was deserted. Roxie had left for the auction house and Wilma had gone to take a couple of residents of the nearby retirement home to doctors' appointments. Kathryn's deepest wish was to sit down in the blessedly quiet house with a full pot of tea and decide what she was going to do next.

Most definitely she was not going to sit and brood. Sure, she had made a mistake, several in fact, but she wouldn't let them ruin her life.

She had just put the water on to boil and was digging out the teapot when the phone rang.

She picked up the receiver before she realized it might be Reid, then she dismissed the thought. Fortifying herself with a deep breath, she said, "Hello?"

"Uh, Kathryn, is that you?" Jill Clevenger's voice wavered uncertainly over the line.

"Yes. Hello, Jill."

"Oh, I'm so glad I caught you before you left for work. I've had my baby," she crowed. "It's a girl!"

Kathryn gasped. "So soon? She's a month early."

Jill seemed too excited to be concerned. "I know, and barely five pounds, but she's healthy. The doctor's keeping her in an isolette for a couple of days for observation, but everything's going to be all right. I just know it."

Jill's bubbling joy was infectious, and Kathryn found herself smiling for the first time in hours. "Congratulations! I'm so happy for you."

"My husband Tim is about to bust his buttons. He's off buying cigars to hand out."

"I'll bet."

"The baby isn't in with me so I can have nonfamily visitors, if you'd like to come by," Jill said, obviously eager to share her good fortune.

"I'll be there," Kathryn promised and hung up. Celebrating a new life today was exactly what she needed. She turned off the stove burner, grabbed her purse and headed for her car.

At the hospital Jill's brown eyes shone with excitement as she told Kathryn the details of her daughter's birth. They had decided to name her Joanna because it meant God's gracious gift, and they had waited so many years for her.

Kathryn rejoiced with her friend, but left when Jill began to grow tired. She slipped out and down the hall to the nursery where she scribbled the name Clevenger on a scrap of paper from her purse and held it up to the window.

Smiling, a nurse rolled a high, plastic-bubbled bassinet to the window so Kathryn could admire its occupant. Despite her tiny size, little Joanna was pink and beautiful with masses of dark hair like her mother's.

"Hello, little one," Kathryn whispered. "Welcome to the world."

The baby wasn't aware of her audience, of course. She slept on serenely, never knowing the turmoil in the heart of the woman who watched the quick rise and fall of her chest as breath passed in and out of her tiny nose.

Kathryn leaned one hip against the waist-high wall beneath the window and crossed her arms at her chest. She thought about all that had happened in the two months since little Joanna had tried to make her early entrance into the world. She treasured a wealth of wonderful memories along with the painful ones of being in love with Reid.

If she concentrated on the positive memories of their fun times together, and with Sean, she could drift along blissfully. She shifted her position restlessly and rubbed her hands up and down her arms. Maybe she should think of the negative things and get over him faster.

Deep in thought Kathryn barely heard the rapid approach of footsteps on the carpeted corridor until she felt her forearm gripped in an iron fist, and she was spun around to face the furious man towering over her.

"Reid," she squeaked.

"So this is where you disappeared to. Jill called me about her baby, said you were on the way here." His gaze shot to the sleeping infant on the other side of the glass, softening a bit, then frosting over when he looked back at Kathryn. "I found your asinine letter of resignation."

Offended, Kathryn threw back her head. "Well, what did you expect?"

"A little consideration for one thing, but maybe that's too much to ask. I can't believe you really did it," he went on, his eyes like silver lances. "You said you'd leave and damned if you didn't. Found out you couldn't make the world a rosy place, after all?"

"What are you talking about?"

Their voices had risen. Down the hall at the nurse's station, a white-capped head came up and a nurse sent them a frowning look. Reid caught the movement and frog-marched Kathryn down the hall to a small waiting room. She tried to jerk her arm away, but he held fast. Once inside the room, he let the door swing shut behind them.

Reid swung her around to face him. He loomed over her, dwarfing everything in the room with his size and towering rage. "I'm talking about you trying to change things. Sean's deafness—or me—whatever was in your mind. You couldn't, so you took off like a scared jackrabbit."

"That's crazy," Kathryn sniffed, finally jerking her arm from his grasp. "I wouldn't change a hair on Sean's head. He's perfect as he is. As for you—" she threw him a scathing glance "—I'd sooner try to transform the Rock of Gibraltar into a marshmallow!" She stalked away from him contemptuously.

Reid's thick brows snapped together. "Then why did you resign and clear out? You could have at least given some notice. You owe me that much."

He was right. Kathryn regretted the way she had left, but there was no other choice. She lifted her chin. "I don't owe you. I'm not stupid. I realized our so-called friendship wasn't going to work out."

"Brilliant deduction. I figured that out, too. Friendship isn't what I want from you."

Kathryn's eyes heated until the gold outshone the green. "You couldn't have made that more obvious.

Maybe I'm slow, but I finally caught on to how you really felt about me, and I decided to leave."

Reid stabbed a hand through his hair. He stared at her, his angry look transforming slowly to one of bafflement. "Well, hell, that doesn't make the least bit of sense. If you knew I was in love with you—"

"In love?" Her eyes popped wide. "I certainly never thought that! You said you didn't want to get involved with me."

He paced away from her then turned back. "I didn't. Hell, I knew you were trouble the first time I ever saw you."

"Thanks."

Reid caught her insulted look and shook his head. "Right away it seemed like everyone in the company flocked to you with their problems."

"They did not!"

"How about the sales rep and his breakup with his girlfriend—to name just one?"

Kathryn glanced away. "Oh, that…" She shrugged. "But there's nothing wrong with wanting to help people, make things a little easier for them."

"No, there isn't, unless it's someone like me."

"Cold and distant, you mean?" she taunted.

The corner of one eye twitched down in a wince. "It was a front. I'd been trudging along for two years on my own, working twelve-hour days, taking care of Sean." He stroked his chin as he gave her a rueful look. "Then you came along…and I tried to keep my distance, tried not to know anything about you."

"You succeeded." Feeling hurt, Kathryn crossed her arms at her waist. She didn't know where he was leading with all this talk. It was possible she should feel elated that he was talking at all, but with Reid, what was the point?

"Oh, really? I noticed you every time you walked past my door. Do you know it takes you exactly three and a half steps to go past?"

Kathryn's eyes rose slowly to meet his. "No."

"Or that when you open the door out to the warehouse, you turn the knob with your right hand and shove it with your hip, pivoting a little on your left foot?"

"Well, I'm right-handed...and I...no, I guess not."

Reid ran his hand around the back of his neck. "Well, I noticed. That and a hundred other things about you, so I tried doubly hard to treat you as impersonally as possible."

Kathryn stabbed a finger in his direction. "Now *that* I noticed!"

"Fat lot of good it did me, especially when you decided to take over Jill's job." He looked her straight in the eyes. "I didn't want you that close."

"No kidding." She should be angry with him, Kathryn told herself, she should be offended, but instead an odd sort of peace was growing inside her.

"And yet I carried you through a flood and rescued a kitten for you and let you hire your roommate and act as my hostess—and thought about committing murder when you flirted with Jared Sykes."

"I didn't flirt!" she protested automatically. The peace of mind was giving way to amazement. Reid never displayed this much of his feelings, except to Sean, whom he loved. Was it possible that...? Nah.

Reid paced away from her again, his long legs carrying him halfway across the room before he turned back. "I saw what was happening, but I didn't want to risk liking you. The more we were together, the more I wanted you. I tried to push you away, but I was fighting myself much harder than I was fighting you. The friendship idea you came up with, though, I thought I could handle that. It worked out for a while—sort of. We had a great time together. You seemed to accept Sean...."

"I do accept him, you six-foot-four-inch, two-hundred-pound dunderhead!" Kathryn practically shouted at him, but her surprise was turning to wonder. Had he really said he loved her?

His next words shot down that hope.

"I was wrong to love you." His blunt-featured face was set in angry lines. "You're going to run out just like—" He stopped and Kathryn finished for him.

"Madeleine?"

"Yeah. She pulled away, ran out emotionally, because of Sean's deafness. You're moving out bag and baggage—"

"Because you're still in love with her and because I'm tired of being compared to her—and always coming up lacking. You've been talking about her for days." Riding on an emotional high, Kathryn stalked over to him. "At the park you pointed out the place where you proposed to her, for goodness' sake! You told those kids playing Frisbee I wasn't Sean's mother in a tone of voice that told me I never would be!"

Genuine surprise shot Reid's brows up. "I'll always love Madeleine—or at least the memory of the way things were at first before Sean got sick and lost his hearing."

Feeling hope draining once again, Kathryn shook her head and turned. Blindly she gazed at a poster of a mother and baby that hung on one pink wall of the waiting room. "I see," she said.

"No, I don't think you do. And I'm doing a god-awful job of explaining myself." Reid drew in a deep breath. "The way I felt about you hit me like a mule's kick between the eyes. I needed some distance, though. That's why I didn't want you to give Sean the magic lessons. The more you were around the more I needed space to decide what to do. I was an idiot. I never planned on falling in love again, much less with someone—"

"Who tries to fix things?" She had heard this before, and Kathryn sent him a resentful glance.

"Well you do, you know. But it's different. Madeleine tried to turn back the clock, make things as they were. You try to help, make people happy."

"It took you long enough to realize that."

"Something else I realized, too—about Madeleine. I was furious with her for what she put us through over Sean. And I was furious with her for dying. I never finished grieving because I . . . couldn't forgive her."

The gruff pain in his voice drew Kathryn around, her face softening in sympathy. Maybe she could never have him, but it agonized her to see him suffer like this. "Those feelings are normal."

"I guess, but I wasn't willing to let go of them until you came along." He shook his head in bemusement. "Rescuing cats, helping people, clowning... The longer I was around you, the more I remembered the good times with Madeleine, times I hadn't thought about in years. It scared me because I didn't want to be at the mercy of my feelings—at the mercy of love—again. Talking about Madeleine put some things in perspective. Remember when Sean got bumped into the lake at the park? You were upset, but you didn't fall apart, just helped clean him off, offered comfort. Madeleine would have rushed him to the hospital emergency room. What I said about you not being his mother came out all wrong—and I hope you'll forgive me—but I let it stand so there would be distance between us and I'd have time to think.''

Never down for long, Kathryn's hopes buoyed again. "That hurt me."

He nodded, his face grim. "I know. God, I'm sorry."

"So by pushing me away, what did you think about?"

He kept his gaze on her. "Us."

"And?"

"I started to think, 'With Kathryn, I could be happy again. She's solid, balanced.'" Reid's hand flew wide in a gesture of hopelessness. "Then *you* started talking about another job."

"I thought you were so in love with her I wouldn't have a chance! I couldn't keep putting myself through torture."

"Well, you were wrong. Understandable since I was so damned stubborn about admitting my feelings." Reid stalked across the room and jerked her into his arms, crushing her mouth beneath his, robbing her of breath, of thought.

Finally he let her surface, gasping. He shook her slightly, his gaze burning over her face. "Don't ever run out on me again. The day Madeleine died, we had an argument about her latest scheme to take Sean to some quack doctor in Mexico. She ran out, jumped in the car and..." His throat seemed to close over the words.

"Had her accident?" Kathryn stood on tiptoe and wrapped her arms around his neck, remembering his urgent calls to see if she had reached home safely. Though she hadn't known, his calling had been a declaration of love. "I'm sorry," she said shakily. "I'll never do that to you again." Then, as the thought struck her, she balled up her fist and punched him on the shoulder. "But you could have told me about that—"

"Ow!" Reid pulled her more tightly against him. "You above all people know it's hard for me to talk about personal problems. But I did tell you just now that I love you." He touched kisses along the side of her jaw and buried his face in her hair. "Say it," he growled. "If I can, you can."

"I love you, Reid," she said clearly, her eyes squeezed shut to hold in the joyful tears. "I have for weeks."

A shuddering sigh gusted from between his lips. "Thank God." He shrugged her away from him and held her chin in the palm of his hand. "Promise me, next time we have a misunderstanding, you'll stay around until it's resolved."

Relief and joy surged through her. She gazed at him, mischief in her eyes. "Careful, Reid, you're about to get yourself involved here."

He grinned down at her. "Too late. I'm already involved. Will you marry me?"

Tears welled from her eyes. "Yes. I thought you'd never ask."

"I thought I'd never ask," he sighed. "You've been one surprise after another, Kathryn Evans, since the day you walked into my company." He lowered his head and kissed her again in a way that told her not all the surprises had been unpleasant. Not by a long shot.

Kathryn stretched to encompass more of him with her arms, pressing her lips to his beloved face and the angle of his freshly shaven jaw.

Happiness and love tangled with her much more earthy feelings of arousal, sending a heady jolt of awareness through her. Her mind skipped through thoughts of what it was going to be like to kiss him, touch him, love him whenever she wanted and know her feelings were returned. After a moment she drew back, though, a slight frown creasing her forehead. "What about gossip at the office, though, Reid? There'll be a lot of it about us."

"Of course. Do you mind?"

She shrugged and glanced at him through her lashes, her cheeks faintly pink. "Yes. I don't want you to look foolish."

"If anybody saw me go roaring out of the office this morning, they'll know I'm a fool, anyway."

"Maybe I should quit when Jill comes back to work."

He frowned, his jaw jutting out. "If you really want to. Just so your new boss is old and decrepit and can't chase you around the desk." Reid paused, running his fingertip absently up and down her cheek. "You could work part-time—at clowning. I know you couldn't make a living at it before, but I think I could manage to support us both for a while. Maybe it's chauvinistic of me, but I'd kind of like you home at least some of the time, and I know Sean would, too. I happen to know my mother would like to get a place of her own, do some traveling, live her own life for a change."

"I think I'd like that." Kathryn sighed contentedly and leaned her head against his chest.

Reid tilted her chin up and kissed her again, and the two of them became lost to the world, until the nurse who'd given them a disapproving look when they'd been arguing pushed the door open. She regarded them with an amused smile while Reid straightened his tie and Kathryn dashed tears from her eyes.

"Are you Reid Darwin?" the nurse asked.

"Yes."

"Mrs. Clevenger in room 502 wants to see you. I told her a six-foot-six man was in the hallway fighting with a little redhead. She said it couldn't possibly be you because you and this lady—" she indicated a blushing Kathryn "—are friends."

"More than friends," he said, drawing Kathryn close with one arm. "So much more, we'll be customers here in a year or so." He swept Kathryn past the grinning nurse. "Reserve your very best room for us."

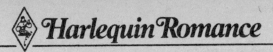
# Harlequin Romance

## Coming Next Month

**#3007   BLUEPRINT FOR LOVE   Amanda Clark**
Shannon West knows that renovating an old house means
uncovering its hidden strengths. When she meets Griff Marek,
an embittered architect—and former sports celebrity—she
learns that love can do the same thing.

**#3008   HEART OF MARBLE   Helena Dawson**
Cressida knows it's risky taking a job sight unseen, but Sir Piers
Aylward's offer to help him open Clarewood Priory to the
public is too good to miss. Then she discovers that he wants
nothing to do with the planning—or with her.

**#3009   TENDER OFFER   Peggy Nicholson**
Did Clay McCann really think he could cut a path through
Manhattan, seize her father's corporation—and her—without a
fight? Apparently he did! And Rikki wondered what had
happened to the Clay she'd idolized in her teens.

**#3010   NO PLACE LIKE HOME   Leigh Michaels**
Just when Kaye's dreams are within reach—she's engaged to a
kind, gentle man who's wealthy enough to offer real security—
happy-go-lucky Brendan McKenna shows up, insisting that *he's*
the only man who can really bring her dreams to life....

**#3011   TO STAY FOREVER   Jessica Steele**
Kendra travels to Greece without hesitation to answer her
cousin Faye's call for help. And Eugene, Faye's husband, seems
grateful. Not so his associate, Damon Niarkos, the most hateful
man Kendra's ever met. What right does he have to interfere?

**#3012   RISE OF AN EAGLE   Margaret Way**
Morgan's grandfather Edward Hartland had always encouraged
the enmity between her and Tyson—yet in his will he divided
the Hartland empire between them. Enraged, Morgan tries to
convince Ty that he's a usurper in her home!

Available in October wherever paperback books are sold, or
through Harlequin Reader Service:

In the U.S.
901 Fuhrmann Blvd.
P.O. Box 1397
Buffalo, N.Y.  14240-1397

In Canada
P.O. Box 603
Fort Erie, Ontario
L2A 5X3

# *Harlequin American Romance*®

## *SUMMER.*

The sun, the surf, the sand . . .

One relaxing month by the sea was all Zoe, Diana and Gracie ever expected from their four-week stays at Gull Cottage, the luxurious East Hampton mansion. They never thought they'd soon be sharing those long summer days—or hot summer nights—with a special man. They never thought that what they found at the beach would change their lives forever. But as Boris, Gull Cottage's resident mynah bird said: "Beware of summer romances. . . ."

Join Zoe, Diana and Gracie for the summer of their lives. Don't miss the GULL COTTAGE trilogy in American Romance: #301 *Charmed Circle* by Robin Francis (July 1989), #305 *Mother Knows Best* by Barbara Bretton (August 1989) and #309 *Saving Grace* by Anne McAllister (September 1989).

GULL COTTAGE—because a month can be the start of forever . . .

---

You'll flip . . . your pages won't!
Read paperbacks *hands-free* with

# Book Mate · I

**The perfect "mate" for all your romance paperbacks**

**Traveling • Vacationing • At Work • In Bed • Studying • Cooking • Eating**

Perfect size for all standard paperbacks, this wonderful invention makes reading a pure pleasure! Ingenious design holds paperback books OPEN and FLAT so even wind can't ruffle pages — leaves your hands free to do other things. Reinforced, wipe-clean vinyl-covered holder flexes to let you turn pages without undoing the strap . . . supports paperbacks so well, they have the strength of hardcovers!

Pages turn WITHOUT opening the strap

SEE-THROUGH STRAP

Reinforced back stays flat

Built in bookmark

BOOK MARK

BACK COVER HOLDING STRIP

10 x 7¹⁄₄ opened
Snaps closed for easy carrying too

Available now. Send your name, address, and zip code, along with a check or money order for just $5.95 + 75¢ for postage & handling (for a total of $6 70) payable to Reader Service to:

Reader Service
Bookmate Offer
901 Fuhrmann Blvd.
P.O. Box 1396
Buffalo, N.Y 14269-1396

Offer not available in Canada
\* New York and Iowa residents add appropriate sales tax

BM-G